VERMILION

All the characters and events portrayed in this work are fictitious.

VERMILION

A Felony & Mayhem mystery

PRINTING HISTORY
First edition (Avon): 1980

Felony & Mayhem edition: 2013

Copyright © 1980 by Nathan Aldyne

All rights reserved

ISBN: 978-1-937384-88-3

Manufactured in the United States of America

Library of Congress Cataloging-in-Publication Data

Aldyne, Nathan.
 Vermilion / Nathan Aldyne. -- Felony & Mayhem edition.
    pages cm
 "A Felony & Mayhem mystery."
 ISBN 978-1-937384-88-3
 1. Gay bars--Massachusetts--Fiction. 2. Valentine, Dan (Fictitious
 character)--Fiction. 3. Lovelace, Clarisse (Fictitious character)--Fiction.
 4. Murder--Investigation--Massachusetts--Fiction. 5. Mystery fiction.
 I. Title.
 PS3551.L346V47 2013
 813'.54--dc23
                          2013044751

For the two Donalds and Louis

The icon above says you're holding a copy of a book in the Felony & Mayhem "Traditional" category. We think of these books as classy cozies, with little gunplay or gore but often a fair amount of humor and, usually, an intrepid amateur sleuth. If you enjoy this book, you may well like other "Traditional" titles from Felony & Mayhem Press.

<hr/>

For more about these books, and other Felony & Mayhem titles, or to place an order, please visit our website at

www.FelonyAndMayhem.com

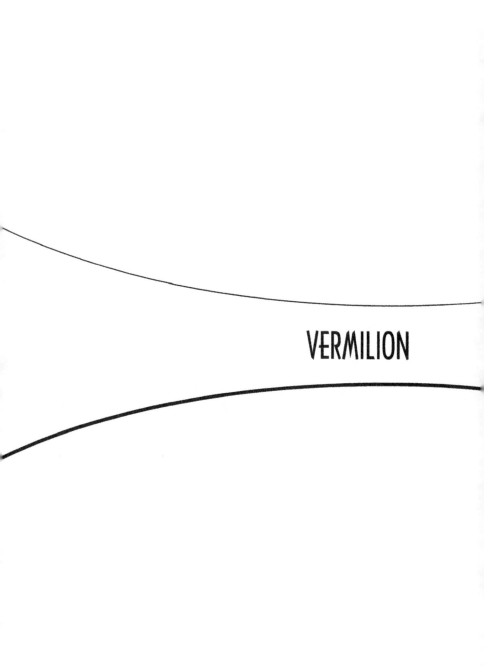

VERMILION

Monday, 1 January

Chapter One

THE FIRST NIGHT of the new year was bitterly cold. A wet chilling wind swept mercilessly down from Quebec. Sheets of snow-filled clouds blotted out the sharp small stars. A white sliver of the waxing moon was lost early in the evening, and never reappeared.

On Marlborough Street, Billy Golacinsky clapped a hand over his chapped lips, and breathed deeply. The cold air sliced through his throat, and beneath the pain was the unmistakable scent of snow. Billy hoped it would hold off an hour, just half an hour more. The unabating wind was punishment enough.

Billy shoved his ungloved balled fists into the pockets of his nylon football jacket. It was a size too large for his slender frame, and the wind cut down his upturned collar and blew up underneath the frayed and stretched waistband. The thin sweatshirt gave some protection but little warmth. Beneath the worn denim, Billy's legs were numbing in the wet wind that funneled down the narrow dark street. He shifted his weight from one foot to the other, but his cheap black sneakers afforded no real protection against the cold.

Billy moved a dozen numbers up the block to stand beneath the one converted gas lamp that had burned out. He leaned uncomfortably against the icy post, and directed his eyes toward Berkeley Street. Marlborough was one-way, and any vehicle that was to pass him would appear at that intersection first.

Tall, narrow brick townhouses lined both sides of the street. Tiny front yards were protected by low cast-iron fences. Windows in the converted buildings across the street from Billy were unlighted, the student inhabitants still away on their Christmas-New Year's holidays. In the darkened windows of a five-story dormitory, Billy studied the reflection of the streetlamps and, higher up, the mirrored black sky. In the few lighted windows on the block, Billy could see broken ceiling moldings, scraggly hanging plants, the wrong side of soiled curtains.

The block of Back Bay demarcated by Arlington and Berkeley streets, Commonwealth Avenue and Marlborough is Boston's principal cruising ground for male hustlers. In better weather, it seems that each lamppost and almost every parking meter is occupied by a slouching insolent young man, while a steady flow of automobiles with attentive drivers makes a stately progress round and round the block.

A car will draw up out of the continuous line beside a fire hydrant. The passenger door falls open, and the nearest young man will pull out of his slouch, and climb in. The car circles the Block once more, and if the young man and the driver cannot agree on a price, the hustler is deposited at the same fire hydrant. But more often, the car proceeds to one of the many dark alleys only minutes distant.

At high summer, the Block is often crowded, but at no time is it ever boisterous. Tourists imagine that the cars are stopping to ask directions. The hustlers, though perhaps acquainted with one another, socialize elsewhere. They move silently from parking meter to lamppost, from lamppost to iron fence. But, on the first day of the new year, Billy Golacinsky was a solitary figure slouching beneath the burned-out lamp.

He'd been on the Block over an hour. Seventeen cars—he'd counted them—had passed, and not one of them had slowed appreciably. Billy's hopes for a warm bed for the night were diminishing, but he steeled himself to at least another hour in the open. Having fallen two weeks behind on the rent on his tiny single room in the Joy Street Chambers, he had been evicted the afternoon before. His clothing and small valuables he had packed in a duffel bag and checked in a bus station locker; the two director's chairs and the green bamboo mat—his only furniture—he had abandoned to the next inhabitant. In his pocket were the key to the bus station locker, his Royal Baths membership card, and a photo ID that gave his real name and age. Secreted in one sneaker was a ten-dollar bill, all the money he had left.

He curled his toes, and the slight unevenness beneath his foot was reassuring. At the last, he could purchase admittance to the baths, and hope to find someone to invite him to share a narrow cot in one of the low-walled cubicles. But this was his last ten, and he had hoped to make at least twenty more tonight. The summer before, Billy thought ruefully, he had often turned sixty dollars before midnight.

Headlights suddenly glared around the corner of Berkeley, and a dark-colored Saab turned down Marlborough. Billy steadied his weight on both feet, placing them wide apart. He relaxed his shoulders, and slipped his frozen hands into the back pockets of his jeans. He thrust out his hips to a prescribed angle, and the practiced hustler's stance was complete. Billy strove to look at once aloof and very much available. As the car drew closer he raised his head erect. The wind drove against his neck, and blew his dry blond hair across his eyes.

The car drew abreast of him. Loud music blared behind the windows raised against the cold. Taking care to retain his posture, Billy glanced warily into the vehicle.

Two young men laughed and talked above the music. Both were short-haired and moustached. Their heavy coats had been unfastened, and their scarves were loosened about their shoulders.

The Saab rolled past. Neither of the men had seen him. Billy's shoulders went slack and he turned his back to the wind. The car swung onto Arlington Street and disappeared.

Swearing aloud, Billy crossed his arms tightly for warmth, and moved to sit on the wide granite stoop of an unlighted building. The heavy balustrade offered some protection from the wind.

He looked up the sidewalk. A man stood unmoving beneath the corner lamp at Berkeley Street, but not in the hustler's stance; he was possibly a mark, at least not competition. Billy looked quickly toward the other end of the street, then back again—now he could see the dog. The man moved toward Billy, his progress halting only because of the evidently recalcitrant animal.

Billy stood, tucked his hands lightly into his jacket, and ambled casually toward the man. He tried to appear as if he were not wretchedly discomforted by the cold.

The tall slender man appeared well built beneath his black pea coat. Sandy blond hair, showing beneath his black knit watch cap, matched the color of his well-trimmed beard. His features were not exceptional, but his expression was one of self-confident easeful strength. A red wool scarf spilled up out of the collar of his coat, wrapped around his neck, and fell over his shoulder. He pulled impatiently on the long leash to hurry the dog along.

Before Billy reached him, the man spoke sharply to the dog and turned around, dragging the animal now in the opposite direction and with equal vigor. Billy thought the man had not seen him; he stepped faster, and slowed only when he came abreast of him.

The bearded man looked over at Billy, knitted his brow curiously, then glanced deliberately away.

"Hi," said Billy. In the light of the streetlamp, Billy guessed the man's age to be thirty.

The man looked over again. "Isn't it a little cold...?"

"A little," Billy replied with a half-smile. The man evidently knew what was going on.

The man stopped and turned to face Billy. He pulled the dog close, wrapping the leash about one leather-gloved hand. His pale blue eyes narrowed. "It's five degrees out here, that's minus fifteen Celsius. Windchill factor of forty below. Is it worth it?"

Taken aback, Billy shuffled his feet, wanting to get from under the man's level gaze; but the hope that the man would pick him up was stronger, and he did not move. The man was young and handsome, but Billy had come across other young and handsome men who craved the excitement of picking up a hustler. Even if this man weren't one of those, perhaps he would simply feel sorry enough for Billy to take him home. He wondered if he shouldn't immediately offer himself for free, but feared putting the man off.

"That a sheep dog?" Billy asked.

"No," said the man, after a slight pause that seemed to mean something, but which Billy couldn't interpret. "It's an afghan." Without another word, the man walked on. Billy followed.

The man stopped again at the corner of Berkeley and Marlborough beneath a light. The afghan wrapped its leash around the trunk of a small, dying tree, to the man's intense displeasure.

"Do you have a cigarette?" Billy asked in a small voice. The insolent slouch had been abandoned back at the burned-out lamp.

The man reached deep into his pocket and pulled out a crushed half-empty pack of unfiltered cigarettes. He handed it to Billy, and then stooped to untangle the afghan from the tree.

Billy tapped a cigarette out of the pack and held it back out to the man.

"Keep 'em," said the man, "I'm quitting."

"Thanks." Billy nodded, and stuffed the pack into his back pocket. He retrieved a pack of matches from the same pocket and tried to light the cigarette. It was impossible in the wind. He gave up but held the cigarette as if it were lit. Billy had to think of something to say that would justify his continuing at the man's side. He had decided to follow when the man crossed the street. The afghan, at last untangled from the tree, nuzzled against Billy's sneaker with the ten-dollar bill inside.

Billy bit his lower lip, and took a drag on the unlit cigarette. The man watched, shook his head and laughed softly. Billy looked up suddenly, brushed the hair from his eyes. "What are you up to?" he blurted.

The man didn't answer. He stepped off the curb, jerking the dog forward. Then he turned, looked directly at Billy and said, in an uninflected and somehow weary voice, "Listen, kid, nobody's out tonight. Nobody's playing. Nobody's buying. Everybody shot his wad last night. Remember? New Year's Eve. John is home with his wife, John is home with his lover, John couldn't get his car started in the cold. John is not going to show up on the Block tonight. Your timing's bad, kid. Go home and get warm."

The man crossed the street, now dragged by the afghan. Billy watched as he moved down unlighted Berkeley Street and turned onto Beacon.

Billy crushed the cigarette in his hand, and wiped the loose tobacco off on his pants. He crossed Berkeley, and stepped a few dozen yards into the alley that ran behind Commonwealth Avenue. He craned his head to search out a particular set of windows half a block down, and cursed to find them dark. He knew people in that apartment, but evidently they weren't in. He returned to his station beneath the burned-out lamp on Marlborough.

Anger, frustration, and humiliation now made him tremble as the cold had not. No car had passed while he talked to the man with the afghan; none appeared now.

A single harsh church bell marked the hour. Billy abandoned the icy post and hurried with sudden resolution to Arlington Street. The man with the dog was right: no one was out looking for trade tonight. Billy felt a fool for having wasted his time in so dismal and uncomfortable a fashion. Despite the cold, a flush of angered heat broke through his frame.

Billy crossed Arlington and stumbled into the darkness of the Public Garden. On the ornate footbridge that crossed

Swan Lake, the first flakes of snow flashed against his face. He burrowed his hands deeper into his pockets and pressed his arms closer to his sides. He ran to the eastern boundary of the garden, sprinted cross Charles Street, and slowed to a brisk tripping walk as he entered the Common. He cut around the baseball field and the tennis courts, and hurried past the black brick tombs of the Revolutionary cemetery. More snow caught on the thickly intertwined branches above him, and blew through the halos of the streetlamps over Boylston Street.

He stopped abruptly when he hit the sidewalk. Melted snow mixed with perspiration dripped down his temples. The sweatshirt stuck uncomfortably beneath his arms.

Traffic here was moderate. High tungsten lights above turned the cold air a feverish amber. Neon signs marked bars and nightclubs in garish pastels. Automobile headlights, storefront fluorescence, and naked white bulbs in the alleyways prevailed at street level.

Directly across from the Revolutionary cemetery was a brightly lighted recessed doorway, above which "Nexus" was spelled out in red neon Deco letters. Several young men, dressed like Billy only more warmly, huddled there, talking, passing a joint, and jerking spasmodically with the cold. All eyes followed any man who entered or departed Nexus, and conversation was momentarily suspended.

Billy dodged the slow-moving traffic and ducked into the shadow of a burned-out building that, despite the cold, still stank of charred wood and water. He pulled a comb from his pocket and ran it quickly through his hair. Then he wiped his face on his nylon sleeve. After retrieving the ten-dollar bill from his shoe, Billy unzipped his jacket and walked slowly to the entrance of Nexus. He had prepared an arrogant smile for the men gathered there, but they had moved off down the street in a laughing group. The smile fell, and Billy blinked the snow from his eyes.

Billy edged through the dark vestibule. The coatroom was not yet opened—the crowd could not be as great as he had hoped.

He stepped cautiously onto the carpeted ramp that spiraled easily down into the large main area of the bar. Involuntarily, Billy paused. The sudden blast of heat, the blaring music from the enormous speakers on either side of him, the pricks of blinding white and silver light off the revolving glitter ball were too great a contrast to cold, silent, dark Marlborough Street. He leaned against a wall until he had adjusted to the changes.

After a time, Billy made his way down the ramp. Below, two bars flanked a darkened stage, used for drag shows and live bands on the weekends. Billy stood at the smaller bar with one sneaker on the brass foot rail. He looked about before ordering.

There were no more than twenty-five patrons in Nexus, most at the other end of the room. He wouldn't be able to make out their faces until the glitter ball was darkened, and the dim red wall lights were brought back on. Billy assured himself that the crowd would have doubled within the half hour.

The bartender, a balding round-faced paunchy man of middle age, wearing a white shirt with a butterfly collar and wide yellow suspenders, was talking casually with two customers at the opposite end of the bar. Billy raised a finger to attract his attention but the bartender didn't see him. Billy looked closely at the customers—a man and a woman. The man was black; he wore a tailored purple suit and a black tie over a ruffled pink shirt. On the collar of the suit jacket was a large diamond stickpin that matched his cuff links, all in heavy gold. The woman wore insubstantial sandals, a pair of unfaded jeans cut off appreciably above the line of her thighs, and a brief white blouse with large red polka dots scattershot over it. Her heavy white-blond hair flared above her ears into long thick ponytails. She was a hooker who, in warmer weather, stationed herself in a particular doorway on the next street over. Billy had never seen her when she was not dressed as Daisy Mae Yokum.

She and her companion laughed at something the bartender said and then slipped off their stools as a disco version of "Ave Maria" rode over the end of the last song. Red, green, and gold lights flashed in time with the music. The couple paused directly beneath the now darkened glitter ball, listened a moment, and on cue erupted into dance. The man moved his feet very little, possibly because of the stricture of his sharply pointed tiny boots, but the woman was all elbows, ankles, and breasts flailing in the heated colorful air. They were the only couple on the floor.

Billy squinted at the dozen tables lining the opposite wall. He made out the shadowy figures of two other hustlers, sprawled in the darkness, also waiting for the crowd. He tightened his stance in the sudden heat of competition.

"What'll it be?" said the bartender, just at Billy's shoulder.

"Miller."

The bartender flipped open a cooler, extracted a bottle and twisted off the lid before sliding it across the bar. Billy held out the ten.

"On the house. Happy New Year," the man said and winked without smiling.

Billy nodded thanks and stuffed the bill back into his pocket. He felt better for having saved the dollar. He could nurse this beer until a man entered who would buy him others; who would want to spend thirty or even forty dollars more after the bar had closed. Billy moved around the corner of the bar to a stool in the shadows. He laid his jacket across the seat, and then swung onto the stool in the approved fashion of hustlers.

By midnight, only about fifty persons had showed up, but the small crowd was lively. The dance floor was never empty, and the single waiter never enjoyed the opportunity to sit with his friends. Billy remained in the shadows. He leaned against the bar, elbows up, drink in one hand, cigarette in the other, legs cast wide apart. He searched every face that passed near him, discounting the regular patrons, the hookers between tricks or just out of the cold, and the four drag queens. That still left more than a dozen older men for him to work on. From long practice Billy could recognize hunger and desperation in a man's eyes from ten paces away in dim red light; he also knew how to disguise the same in himself—with lowered lids and a seductive, apparently unconscious half-smile.

Billy lit another cigarette. He had nursed his beer one hour by the clock. He guzzled the last of the warm liquid, and set the bottle disconsolately on the bar. Another Miller's took its place immediately.

Billy looked around at the bartender.

"Your timing's good tonight," said the man dryly.

"Who bought it?" demanded Billy.

The bartender shrugged. "An admirer. Anonymous—at least for right now."

Billy drank this second beer much more quickly, and stared about trying to guess which man had sent it over. After a bit, he gave this over as not worth his trouble—it was unlikely the man would go away unintroduced.

Three free beers later Billy was weary and woozy. It was past one; the bar would close in less than an hour. Before then he must secure a bed for the night and money for the following day.

Billy looked around. The crowd was not larger, but was differently composed. Daisy Mae had left and returned with an undistinguished overweight man about fifty. He was now purchasing at least a third set of hard drinks. Daisy Mae sipped hers, and abandoned it half finished, while encouraging her companion to gulp his down. She coyly brushed her breasts against his chest while whispering—licking—in his ear. The man's eyes were bright and distracted. He dragged Daisy Mae onto the dance floor and, ignoring the disco beat, held her in a slow embrace. She accommodated him, bending slightly forward and jutting her Parker House posterior far behind her. When her partner lurched drunkenly, Daisy Mae fell roughly against a drag queen who was impersonating a TWA stewardess. The stewardess turned heatedly on the comic-book hooker. Those around them left off dancing and grinned expectantly, calling for a fight.

Billy wanted to move closer for a better view, but found he was now too drunk to stand easily. He leaned back and yawned, for the first time in the evening indifferent to how he ended up.

"I don't know if I should buy you another drink."

Billy looked to his side. His unfocused vision smeared white hair and a round pink-cheeked face across his brain. He turned back to the fight.

The man signaled the bartender and received another beer. He handed it to Billy.

"Drink up and we'll go."

Billy took the sweating bottle and looked slowly up at the older man. Billy stared at his face and found it more unhandsome than he was accustomed to. The man wore a heavy overcoat over a dark brown double-knit leisure suit. Beneath the off-white dress shirt, a thin gold chain was hung about his wrinkled pink neck.

"Thirty-five," Billy said carefully, trying to sound sure of himself and sober.

The thin-lipped mouth pursed. The bright eyes dropped down Billy's body appraisingly. "Twenty," the man said.

Billy swiveled the bar stool around, and stared at the clock behind the bar. Nexus would close in twenty-five minutes. He raised the beer and drank it down in several long gulps.

"All right," he said. He dropped unsteadily to the floor and the man gripped his arm. Billy pulled away and struggled into his jacket.

Above the disco version of "Auld Lang Syne" there was a hoarse shriek. The bartender rushed past Billy, leaping into the crowd on the dance floor. The man with the white hair and pink cheeks led Billy up the ramp.

From the top, Billy turned and stared into the bar. The crowd in the center of the dance floor had pulled back a little. The bartender had been knocked to the floor. The TWA stewardess had ripped off Daisy Mae's blouse, and tossed it to a girlfriend, who was dressed as a geisha. Daisy Mae shrieked in terrible anger.

The man touched Billy's arm and guided him out into the cold New Year's night.

Tuesday, 2 January

Chapter Two

PROFESSOR PHILIP Lawrence stood on his front porch and stared across the snow-covered street at the row of hemlocks that screened the house of his neighbors across the way. His breath crystallized in sharp puffs, and he squinted angrily in the cold glare. A pile of someone's discarded clothing had been spilled out onto the side of the road. Mercifully, the heap had been dumped not onto his own lawn, but onto the property of Mario Scarpetti, fourth-term representative to the Massachusetts legislature.

Pulling his wide-brimmed black felt hat down further and wrenching his collar up about his neck, Lawrence moved resolutely down the sidewalk. He was wrapped in a black greatcoat and carried a black leather attaché case in one kid-gloved hand. His full auburn beard was stiffening in the cold air. The marred landscape rankled him and he knew that if he did not retrieve and dispose of the trash it would be there to annoy him when he returned from a full day of classes. The Scarpettis had money and a certain peculiar prestige, but little sense of pride in the appearance of their neighborhood.

As he crossed the road, powdery snow clouded up about his black boots. From his coat pocket he retrieved a pair of glasses, thin gold-rimmed spectacles with smoked amber lenses. As soon as he had them on, the lenses fogged. With well-practiced but grudging patience, he wiped the glass clear with a white starched kerchief. He stood on the sidewalk a few feet from the row of hemlocks, and looked down through the dense evergreen foliage. His mouth loosened and fell slightly open.

"Jesus *Christ*...!" he exclaimed.

The head of the corpse, its face turned modestly into the snow, was obscured by the deep-green branches of the hemlocks. Without hesitation Lawrence bent over and pulled back the foliage.

The man was young, no more than twenty, Lawrence surmised. He was sprawled on his side, arms and legs tangled in the broken lower branches of two of the trees. Above the right temple, the thick blond hair was caked with blood. A thin stream had frozen like a bright red frame around the corpse's staring clouded eye.

Lawrence let go of the branches, sifting snow over the bruised head, and stood erect. The boy wore a too-large nylon football jacket, dark blue with yellow piping; the insignia was of a high school in Pennsylvania. A thin green sweatshirt was still tucked carefully into thin faded denim jeans. The corpse's feet, in dirty white athletic socks and worn black sneakers, pushed against the black trunk of one of the hemlocks.

Lawrence pushed aside some of the higher branches, and looked across the expanse of inclined whited lawn, thick with bare lindens and blue spruce, up to the Scarpetti's house. The structure was a solid three stories, squarish, covered with cream stucco. An ornate parapet running about the edge of the roof was the only decoration on the otherwise severe 1920s design. Nothing stirred behind the windows on the near side of the house.

The snow on the lawn was unmarred. Lawrence turned to look briefly up and down the road, which ended in a cul-de-sac two houses beyond. There were no footprints near the boy's body, but a faint set of tire tracks came up from the highway to the spot, and was repeated going down again. The boy had evidently been dumped shortly after the snow began to stick.

Professor Philip Lawrence smiled with pleasure as he contemplated informing Representative Mario Scarpetti that the body of a young man had been deposited beneath his hemlocks. He glanced once more at the corpse, and then stepped through the screen of evergreens, heading toward the house.

Chapter Three

DANIEL VALENTINE punched a key on the cash register. The bell pinged sharply as the "$1.00" tab popped up into the tiny glass window and the drawer slid open. He smoothed the bill out and pushed it into the proper compartment. Before closing it, Valentine reached into the back of the drawer and extracted matches and a fresh pack of Lucky's.

Valentine opened the cigarettes and took one out. He leaned his elbows lazily on the highly polished bar and smoked sedately, consciously enjoying this slow part of the evening. In less than an hour, Bonaparte's regular crowd would begin its erratic but inevitable buildup. He sighed and dragged deep on the Lucky; he was weary and the 2:00 A.M. closing seemed about four days away. For the fifth time in ten minutes, he swept his eyes across the room for a head count.

A little down from the register two men in business suits talked quietly and laughed softly as they sipped at a third round of rye. In a shadowed corner stood three other men, who were regulars at Bonaparte's.

In rattan chairs set among the jungle of palms in the room behind the mirrored bar two more men pursued a low-voiced serious argument, the same discussion that had occupied them in an identical manner—in the same chairs, across the same table—over the past couple of months. The walls of this back room were a dark rich green. Six more rattan chairs were grouped around three more glass-topped wicker tables. In the corner was a lacquered baby grand.

Valentine checked his watch. Trudy, scheduled to play at the piano from ten to two, was late, but not much later than usual. Trudy maintained that she couldn't tell the time on a digital clock.

Valentine looked across the room, through the opened white louvered doors. The foyer was empty but for Irene at her station in the coat checkroom. Irene was a plump woman in her sixties, who wore her white hair pulled severely back into a bun at the nape of her neck. Large round rhinestone-studded bifocal glasses perched at the bridge of her thin red nose. Alert but motionless, hands resting on the lower half of the Dutch door, Irene stared ahead as if she were momentarily expecting to witness a bloody murder on the staircase that led to the dance floor above. She did not notice Valentine's wink.

Valentine mixed himself a tonic water and lime.

Bonaparte's had changed little since it was converted in 1925 from a private residence into a speakeasy. Discreetly situated on the quiet edge of Boston's Bay Village, the bar had carefully established and perpetuated a reputation as a quiet decorous gathering place for the city's wealthy and older gay men.

The room in which Valentine worked had been the original parlor of the townhouse. The ornate wainscoting and ceiling medallion remained and panels of lightly tinted mirror had been placed into the four walls. From the bar Valentine was able to watch all who entered and mingled in the Mirror Room or sat in the rattan chairs in the shadowy Wicker Room behind.

Valentine looked across the room at his reflected image. He studied himself carefully and frowned. He had lost some weight, he thought. Having worked long hours almost every night during the Christmas holidays, he had not been able to visit the gym in the past two weeks. He usually went on Mondays, Wednesdays, Fridays, and Sunday afternoons for a rigorous workout on the Universal gym machine, a half hour run around the track and a final few laps in the pool. He didn't much like this exhausting exercise—in fact, he hated it—but it kept him in shape. He took a swallow of his tonic and lime and resigned himself to the resumption of the schedule on the following day.

Valentine had begun keeping bar for Bonaparte's five years before, as a weekend supplement to his meager salary as a prison counselor at the Charles Street Jail. However, after informing the Boston *Globe* that the sheriff of Suffolk County, whose house immediately adjoined the prison, had paid ten thousand dollars of taxpayers' money for his living room draperies, Valentine had been fired from his state job. He had got this information not through his connection with the prison, but from the sales representative of the company that had provided the material, with whom he had had a brief affair. Valentine had been privately assured that he would regain his position at the prison as soon as the sheriff was out of office, and he had decided to work full-time at Bonaparte's until then. It had been a disappointment that the man had been reelected, but now there was some hope that he would die in office.

Tending the main bar at Bonaparte's brought in better money than the Charles Street Jail, and the hours were more congenial, but Daniel Valentine still wished for his old post. If questioned, he always denied it, but the truth was that he had much satisfaction in helping prisoners adjust both to captivity and release. Friends had urged Valentine to take one of the positions that were open in other Massachusetts prisons, at Concord or Walpole, but Valentine met these suggestions with unfeigned horror, for it was unthinkable that he should work outside the city. "I get the shakes," he would shudder, "just thinking about the suburbs, and I haven't seen the open countryside in five years..."

From beneath the bar Valentine pulled the late edition of the Boston *Globe*. He spread the paper out and was taken aback by the headline in the lower right-hand corner of the front page. Bold black letters cried, SLAIN YOUTH DISCOVERED ON STATE REP'S LAWN and in smaller print, "Rep. Scarpetti Blames 'Homosexual Conspiracy.'" With knitted brow Valentine darted down the column of text, reading uneasily. Mario Scarpetti had led the fight in the House, just that past November, to defeat a bill, already passed in the state Senate, that would have made unlawful discrimination against homosexuals in the matter of public housing and employment. He was an ignorant, loudmouthed, and powerful enemy of Boston's gay community.

"The body of a young man was discovered early this morning on the lawn of State Rep. Mario Scarpetti's suburban home. Apparently placed there sometime during the night or early morning, the victim has been identified as William A. Golacinsky, nineteen, of Harrisburg, Pa. The young man's father was contacted early this morning..."

And further down:

"Police sources revealed that Golacinsky was a known hustler, or male prostitute, in the Boston area, and had been arrested only three weeks ago on a charge of soliciting. The charges in that case were dropped..."

"'It's all part of the homosexual conspiracy,' Rep. Scarpetti angrily stated this morning at an impromptu press conference at his home. 'The homosexual element in this city elected a human sacrifice, and put him on my lawn to crucify me. This is just an attempt to smear my good name. If they want to kill their own kind let them do it. All the better for Boston, but let them dump their garbage somewhere else.'"

Valentine drew his fingers into a fist.

"Police Commissioner Joseph O'Brien stated that his department has no suspects as yet but that a full and thorough investigation has been launched. Contacted by phone this morning, O'Brien said that 'it appears to be more than coincidence that the deceased, a known homosexual, was left on Mario's [Rep. Scarpetti's] lawn.'"

Valentine was about to turn the page to the continuation of the story, when a well-manicured hand reached over and pushed the paper aside. Valentine looked up.

The man on the other side of the bar was clean shaven, with a strong prominent square jaw, and a thin hard colorless mouth. His deep-set eyes were dark but shallow-focused; his dark hair was close-cut and wavy. Beneath the open topcoat of good material and cut, he wore a gray suit, finely tailored and well-fitted to his tall muscular frame.

Well, considered Valentine, *this one must work out on Tuesdays and Thursdays too.* He stared at the man, but said nothing.

The man reached into his inside coat pocket and produced a wallet. He flipped it open in an automatic, practiced manner. Pinned to one leaf was a badge and an identification card encased in cracked clouded plastic. Valentine glanced at it and then back to the man's face, no longer wondering why the dark eyes were shallow-focused. The policeman's serious expression was as practiced as his movements.

"Lieutenant Searcy," the man said and flipped the wallet closed. "Police Lieutenant William Searcy," he added, and dexterously the wallet disappeared. The voice was flat and uninflected, as if he feared giving something away by tone.

"Valentine," said Daniel, matching the flat tone. "Daniel Valentine—I'm the bartender here."

Searcy's mouth creased into a frown and he seated himself to face Valentine. He took a small piece of paper from another pocket and cupped it in his hand, away from Valentine. He rested his elbows on the bar and looked briefly about. "Slow night," he said.

Valentine rolled his eyes. "What can I do for you?" he asked.

"I need information."

One of the men further down raised two fingers and Valentine turned to pour another round of rye. In a moment he came back to Searcy.

"Would you like a drink?"

"You may not have guessed it, but I'm on duty."

Valentine sighed. "It's on the house."

Searcy considered a moment. "Bourbon, on the rocks."

Valentine smiled for the first time. From beneath the bar he took a coffee cup, scooped ice into it, and poured in the liquor. He placed it on a saucer and slid it across to the detective. "You're not the only cop who's ever been in here 'on duty.'"

The piece of paper cupped in the policeman's hand snapped face-up onto the bar. Valentine picked the photograph up.

"Ever see this kid in here?"

The picture was in high-contrast black and white: a young man with straight light hair and mottled skin. The coarse unmemorable features were slack and when Valentine looked more closely he saw that a good portion of the forehead had been airbrushed and the eyes painted open. He looked up at Searcy.

"Who is it?"

"You tell me."

Valentine glanced at the photograph again and shrugged. He placed it on the bar between them, turning it so that the blank painted eyes stared at the detective.

"Never saw him before. Is he a desperate character?"

"Not anymore." Searcy took a swallow of his drink.

Valentine blinked but said nothing for a moment. "William A. Golacinsky?" he asked finally.

"You just said you didn't know him."

"I don't," Valentine said as he tapped the newspaper. "But I *have* seen the *Globe*." He lit another cigarette.

"We're trying to trace his movements, find out where he was last night."

"He wasn't with me—not my type," said Valentine. "Perhaps he spent the evening debating homosexual rights with Representative Scarpetti."

"He was a hustler."

"The charges got dropped," said Valentine.

Searcy glanced up quickly. "What do you mean?"

"Nothing," shrugged Valentine. "But why are you asking around here? He was killed out in the suburbs, wasn't he? Horrible things happen to you in the suburbs—"

"The kid was a hustler in Boston, and it's not likely that on a blue-ass cold night in January he was out working the streets of Malden and Medford."

"Maybe he didn't go to a bar at all," suggested Valentine mildly.

"Well, Mr. Valentine," retorted Searcy, "we won't know that until we've checked all the bars where a cheap hustler might have gone last night."

Valentine stabbed his cigarette out in an ashtray. "Look around you, Lieutenant. Check the place out."

Searcy's dark flat eyes scanned the Mirror Room, looked briefly into the Wicker Room, and then returned to Valentine.

"Does this look like the Greyhound station? Do you see any pimply hustlers leaning against the wall?"

"Maybe it's too early."

Valentine spoke contemptuously. "Hustlers don't come to Bonaparte's."

"The men who come here can toss away thirty, fifty dollars on a hustler like it was money for the meter," argued Searcy.

"Sure," Valentine agreed, "a lot of men who come here can afford it. Some of them do—but they don't do it here. You won't find a hustler in here, not the kind you're looking for anyway. The kind of women that you might pick up on a corner in the Combat Zone you won't find in the Copley Plaza bar, and it's the same thing here."

Searcy stood. "But it's not impossible that Golacinsky stopped in here last night, just for a drink, nothing else."

"Maybe he did," smiled Valentine, "I had last night off."

Searcy looked at Valentine for a long moment. His flat eyes glistened. "Then why in the hell didn't you tell me that five minutes ago? Christ—well, who was working here?"

"Jack."

"Where is Jack now?"

"He works the dance floor upstairs, but when I'm off he's down here."

Searcy grabbed the photograph, and glanced behind him. "Do I go up those stairs?"

"*You* don't. I'll take the picture up and show him. Police give Jack amnesia. He'll tell me if he knows anything."

Valentine took the photograph from Searcy's hand and crossed the room. He stopped at the double doors and turned.

"Lieutenant?"

"Yes?"

"No entrapments while I'm gone, OK?" He winked, and whipped up the stairs.

Searcy rubbed his mouth and turned back to the bar. The man sitting nearest him glanced over his body with interest. Searcy returned a frigid stare, and the man looked away, but unembarrassed. Searcy eased back onto the stool. He glanced into a panel of mirror behind the bar, looking the place over in the reflection.

His gaze went no further than the foyer, trapped by the woman he saw there. She was tall and leggy beneath a mahogany-brown fur coat. The garment was cut in the 1940s style, with padded shoulders and wide cuffs. In one gloved hand she carried a brown leather envelope, its bulging contents straining the latch. She tucked this securely under one arm and peeled off her gloves, stuffing them into one pocket. She snatched off her fur skullcap; a great mane of hair cascaded in soft black waves beneath the dull red light of the foyer. She shoved the hat into the other pocket, paused a moment and then pulled hat and gloves out and stepped over to the checkroom. Irene, her eyes still locked on the stairway, absently accepted the articles. Not waiting for her ticket, the woman moved into the bar.

Searcy straightened as she approached. He turned from the mirror, swerving smoothly about on his stool. Midway across the room the woman stopped and looked casually about. Her cheeks were flushed with cold. She had strong even features, large dark blue eyes accented with blue eye shadow, and a full sensual mouth carefully tinted with pale coral lipstick.

The woman noted Searcy briefly, but without discernible reaction. She dropped the heavy envelope onto the stool next to him and unhooked the large buttons on her coat. The fur fell open to reveal large breasts beneath a tailored, expensive blue work shirt, blue jeans tight-belted around a slender waist and hips. The jeans were tucked into knee-high brown leather riding boots. Seating herself, the woman did not gather the coat about her hips, but allowed the fur to dangle freely. She propped her elbows on the bar and appeared to relax. Her eyes flicking to the mirror caught and held Searcy's gaze.

She ran a slender hand through her luxuriant hair. Searcy noted an incongruous adhesive bandage across her knuckles.

"Cut yourself?" Searcy asked.

The woman glanced at her hand, then at Searcy. "I was mugged." Then she smiled. "I'm Clarisse," she said, and nodded in a friendly and uncoy fashion.

Searcy laughed. "My name's Searcy."

"Oh," she laughed. "'Circe?' You turn men into swine, I guess—well, so do I," she added huskily.

"Wait a minute..." he began testily.

She saw with some surprise that he didn't get the joke. "*Cir-ce*," she said carefully. "In *The Odyssey*. Circe turned men into swine. But perhaps that's not the way you spell it."

He spelled his name for her.

"Not the same," she said, adding with a smile, "If this place had a bartender, I'd buy you a drink and apologize."

"Apology accepted." Searcy relaxed again. "Call me Bill."

Clarisse lifted the weighty leather envelope onto the bar and flipped the latch. A bundle of legal papers poured out messily, along with three packs of cigarettes, different brands, a tube of lipstick, several dozen keys on a large ring, and a battered box of adhesive bandages. Clarisse selected the opened pack of Kools and then shoved the contents back into the envelope, struggling for a moment to close the latch. Searcy reached to help and she secured it.

"You're a treasure," she said, and tapped a cigarette out of the pack.

While Searcy beat his pockets for matches Clarisse suddenly leaned past him over the bar and snatched up a pack of matches from a basket beside the cash register. Her breasts brushed against his arm. Sitting comfortably back, she lit her cigarette, drew the smoke deep into her lungs and released it slowly from her mouth. She tossed her thick black hair and looked about the bar, noting each man in the room, evidently unconcerned whether the conversation were pursued by Searcy or not.

"Have you ever been in here before?" asked Searcy.

Clarisse tilted her head. An expression of boredom crept across her mouth. "I've heard better lines on the six A.M. farm report."

"No, what I mean is…well, you know, this is a gay bar."

"Oh," she said blandly. "Is there a sign? I must have missed it." She turned her profile to him.

Searcy paused, trying to decide whether she was being sarcastic or not. "Listen," he went on carefully, "I have to finish up some business here and after I'm done, would you like to go somewhere else for a drink?"

"If this is a gay bar, Mr. Searcy," said Clarisse with a small smile, "what are you doing here trying to pick up a woman?"

"I told you, I have business here, with the bartender. He's upstairs right now. After he comes back we could go over to the Howard Johnson's 57 Club. It's just up the street."

"It's too cold for ice cream."

"No, I meant—"

Before he could finish, Valentine came down the stairs and crossed back behind the bar. He dropped the photograph onto the bar between Searcy and the woman. She picked it up.

"Jack's never seen him."

Searcy shrugged. "I'll leave the print. Show it around and call me if you hear anything." Searcy handed Valentine a cheaply printed business card.

Pocketing the card, Valentine took a glass, filled it halfway with chunks of ice and then poured in two fingers of good scotch. The woman wrapped a hand around it but did not drink.

Searcy was confused by the woman's presence in the bar and now the bartender's evident familiarity with her—though they had not spoken. Yet he could not resist making one more attempt: "Well, I guess you don't want to have that drink with me..."

She looked at him. "Are you a policeman?"

"I'm a detective."

Clarisse lifted the cup Searcy had been drinking from and passed it beneath her nose. She set it back in the saucer.

"I see you're on duty," she said, then more softly, "Maybe some other time."

Searcy nodded harshly.

"Anything else, Lieutenant?" asked Valentine.

"No. Just call me if you get anything."

Valentine lit a cigarette. "You know, Lieutenant, you're wasting your time in here. A nineteen-year-old hustler would never come in Bonaparte's. He'd go to Nexus, or one of the bars in the Zone. If I hear anything I'll call you, but don't sit by the phone."

Searcy rested one large hand on the bar, rhythmically tapping his thumb against the wood. "Let me tell you one thing, Valentine, I don't care if somebody knocks off a hustler every night, but when I'm assigned to a case I check everything. Scarpetti's down our necks like—"

Valentine cut in sharply. "What Scarpetti says is bullshit. It's good press."

The policeman's flat black eyes stared hard at Valentine.

Chapter Four

"EVER RUN INTO that one on Charles Street?" asked Clarisse.

"No," replied Valentine, "but I know the type. Double trouble—"

"He was cute for a cop though."

Valentine cringed. "You don't call somebody like Searcy 'cute.' He's 'ruggedly handsome,' as *Viva* would say."

"Nice touch—those circles under his dark intense eyes. 'A good cop never sleeps.'"

"A good cop doesn't guzzle liquor when he's on duty."

"Just one drink though, wasn't it, Val?"

"It wasn't his first. He didn't have to tell me he was drinking bourbon. I can smell cheap liquor at twenty paces in a chocolate factory. I was probably the first bartender that didn't pour him the house brand."

"It's a hard life when you're a cop," sighed Clarisse.

Valentine looked up. "Why are you making excuses? Your cold shoulder could have sunk the *Titanic*."

"He was OK. I just didn't like the way he came on. I had to use a forklift to get his eyes up above my tits."

"It's no wonder. They must have been practically in his lap."

"It didn't matter," said Clarisse, and ran a long finger around the rim of her glass so that it whistled shrilly, "especially since I've taken a vow of chastity."

"Is that what you told the insurance man you met at the Laundromat last week? You went off with him and let my underwear melt in the dryer."

"It's a recent vow," said Clarisse. "Besides," she added, after a sip of scotch, "he wasn't insurance, he was mutual funds. And we didn't do anything anyway."

"Nothing?"

"At least nothing I thought was worth putting down in my diary for that day."

"Clarisse," said Valentine earnestly, "I'm your best friend in all this large cold city, and I've got to tell you—"

"What?"

"You've got as much chance to bed Searcy as you do me."

"What do you mean?" she demanded.

"Not to slap on a label, but get out the glue: Lieutenant Searcy of Boston's Finest is a 'Lady of the Secret Sorrow.'"

Clarisse's blue-rimmed eyes narrowed. "A what?"

"A closet case. I could be wrong, I was wrong once before. But the eyes are always a giveaway, and Lieutenant Searcy's eyes gave him away."

"Val, you think every man in Boston walks the streets with a splint in his sleeve, to hold up his limp wrist. There's probably a couple of good-looking straight men left somewhere in Boston—though I wish somebody'd point 'em out to me. Besides, I didn't want to marry the man, I just wanted to see what he looked like—with his jacket off."

Valentine was suddenly called to mix half a dozen drinks for men newly arrived. When he returned to Clarisse he found her fingering the photograph that Searcy had left.

"Strange eyes," she said.

"They're painted on. It's a morgue photograph."

Clarisse dropped the print. "Is this Mr. Scarpetti's little friend in the bushes?"

"Yep." Valentine retrieved the picture and stuffed it into the breast pocket of his shirt.

"I was listening to the radio, and I heard something about Mario Scarpetti and a hustler. For a minute there I thought he was announcing he had left his wife for the tender embrace of a sixteen-year-old boy."

"He was nineteen," said Valentine.

"And he was also dead."

Disco music filtered down from the jukebox upstairs, and Trudy was an hour late. Valentine cleared a sink of dirty glasses and Clarisse read about the late William A. Golacinsky.

There was sudden five-fingered pressure on her arm. Clarisse looked up to a man with raised eyebrows and wide melancholy eyes. He was less than thirty-five, clean shaven, with a ruddy complexion. He removed his hand from her arm and smiled apologetically.

"Miss Lovelace?" he asked.

Clarisse nodded, and could not take her eyes from his raised brows. In her mind she screamed, *Go down! Go down!* but they did not, and his wide melancholy eyes grew bigger and sadder.

"You remember me, don't you?"

Clarisse knitted her brow. "I'm afraid...oh yes, I'm sorry." She sat up, and trailed a sharp-pointed nail down his white cambric shirt. "'Two bedroom garden apartment, large living room with marble fireplace, full and half bath, elegant Union Park. $450 a month, all utilities.' I don't remember your name though."

"Griffith," the man smiled. "I was wondering if the lease had been drawn up yet. I went by the realty office twice last week, but you were out both times. I phoned the other days. You weren't in then either."

Clarisse reached over and spilled the contents of the leather envelope across the bar. Without hesitation she reached in the jumbled pile and pulled out a clipped sheaf of papers. "Here it is, Mr. Griffith." The rest she laboriously stuffed back into the envelope. Griffith pressed his thumb gallantly on the latch.

"I apologize for the delay. Everything can be done right now, and Valentine will get you whatever you're drinking."

Valentine pushed a Heineken across the bar.

Clarisse scanned the original, explained several passages briefly, and asked her client to make sure all was in order. She sat silently by while he read through the document. Clarisse fished a pen from her coat pocket, and Griffith initialed and signed both copies beneath her dexterous, pointing finger. He was pleased, and his eyebrows rose another quarter of an inch.

Clarisse looked away. "I was going to call you today, but life is hard when you're a real estate broker. One of my buildings burned to the ground last night, and the arson squad and I have been sifting through wreckage all day."

Griffith nodded sympathetically, and expressed the hope that no one was injured in the fire.

Clarisse shook her head, handed him his copy of the lease and shoved the other back into the envelope. Once again she struggled with the catch. "Twenty-five people homeless, but not a scratch on any of 'em. I think the commissions just aren't worth the long hard hours. Not to mention the heartache. Well, stop by the office and Richie will give you the keys. You'll love Union Park."

Griffith thanked her and wandered away. When Clarisse turned she found Valentine setting a fresh drink before her. "I have never heard such a series of bald lies in my life," he said. "*What* fire?"

"Actually, there *was* a fire last night, but it was in *my* building, just after I got in. The awful little boy who lives upstairs set fire to his father's collection of matchbooks, and they had to throw it in the bathtub to put it out."

"That's not exactly twenty-five people homeless."

"Well, the father was in the bathtub at the time, how's that?"

"Not good enough," said Valentine, "and what was all that about a 'hard life,' and 'long hours,' and what was it—oh yes, 'heartache.' *Heartache?*"

"It's a tough racket. You get hardened."

Valentine laughed. "Maybe if you ever worked an eight-hour day, you'd—" He broke off suddenly, and stared blankly across the room.

"What's wrong?"

He looked at Clarisse a moment before he spoke. "I *have* seen that kid."

Clarisse looked behind her. "Which one?"

Valentine tapped the pocket containing the morgue photo. "Poor little Mr. Golacinsky."

"You told that cop you'd never seen him before."

"He was asking if I had ever seen him in here—and of course I hadn't."

"Then how do you know him?"

"I don't know, but I have seen him. Recently, too. Read what he was wearing when they found him."

Clarisse ran her finger down the column. "Nylon football jacket...jeans, torn sneakers." She looked up. "Maybe he just froze to death."

Valentine blinked. "He was on the Block last night."

"Valentine, you are *not* going to tell me that while I am languishing between freshly laundered percale sheets, that you are out on the street looking for *trade*?"

"I wasn't cruising the Block, I was out there walking your dog. So Veronica Lake and I were going down Marlborough and there was this poor kid, just about frozen to a lamppost, trying to look seductive when it's ten degrees below zero."

"You talked to him?"

Valentine nodded and leaned over the bar toward her. "He wanted me to pick him up. He asked if Veronica Lake were a sheep dog." They both laughed. "I wasn't paying, I wasn't going to take it for free either. I told him to go on home, he was wasting his time."

"What did he do?"

Valentine shrugged. "I don't know. I left him there. I took Veronica Lake back to your place. You still weren't there, so I

went on home. He was dressed just like the paper says, but..."
He removed the photo from his pocket and placed it atop her
glass. "...his eyes were softer than they are here. The way it
looks now, maybe I *should* have taken him home."

"What was he like? Hoodlum, or what?"

Valentine stood erect. "He tried to be tough, I guess. He
didn't make much of an impression. Innocuous. Look, I didn't
even remember him when that cop stuck his picture under my
nose."

Valentine moved away. Clarisse picked up the photograph,
and turned it in the light. She set it down with a small grimace.
She took a swallow of her scotch and lit another cigarette.
Valentine returned.

"Well, are you going to call Searcy? Tell him what you
know?"

"Not this minute. He said he'd be back. I'd rather not—"
Valentine's attention was drawn to the foyer. Clarisse leaned
over a little and looked in the mirror.

"Well," said Valentine, "maybe Trudy'll have time for one
full set before last call."

In the hallway Trudy, her back to the Mirror Room,
unbelted and unzipped her black fur coat in a frenzy of elbows
and shoulder blades. Her head bobbed rapidly as she spoke to
Irene, who paid no attention at all, but stared around the piano
player to the stairway.

Trudy's clinging silk dress set off her shapely supple figure.
She was short, slender, and celebrated for her legs, which
Valentine contended would have precipitated a coronary of jeal-
ousy in Betty Grable. Through cycles of world fashion, Trudy's
skirts remained hemmed three inches above her dimpled knees.
She always wore green—dress, nylons, heels, and accessories.
This unity of color in her dress was offset by the array of wigs
she owned, in all various shades and styles. Her own hair was
reported to be shining white, but even Irene hadn't seen it in
twenty years. Trudy had three grown sons; her wife had died
eighteen months back. Her real name was Sidney Robert White

and she had, as Valentine often said, "the shape of Dolores Del Rio and the face of Charles Laughton." Trudy turned, and twisted her lumpish little face coyly.

Shoulders back, arms tight at her side, she flew from the foyer to the bar. She dropped her green-dyed alligator clutch and her green gloves onto the bar beside Clarisse's leather envelope, and held out her hand for the gin fizz that Valentine had already prepared.

"I think I'm late," she began, and sipping at the drink, held up a hand to prevent Valentine from speaking. She turned her head aside, closed her eyes and spoke quickly, in the undisguised voice of a man in late middle age. She took little bird-sips of the gin fizz between sentences. "First it was the car. Wouldn't start. Wouldn't even roll downhill. Telephone booth didn't have a directory. Couldn't call a garage. It already had three tickets on the door. Four cabs went by, wouldn't pick me up. I was just about to jump out in front of number five when a drunk came by, stepped on my heel and broke it. Had to run limping up the Hill. Little boy—should have been in bed—threw a sandwich at me. Put on another heel, waited for the glue to dry, then had to spray-paint it. Ran all the way down the hill again. Caught the subway. Man accused me of murdering his first wife. Here I am, probably not more than two minutes late. How about another gin fizz?"

"Life's hard," said Clarisse gently.

Trudy idly twirled the overturned photograph with one long green nail. "Sometimes I wish I'd just dedicated myself to the kitchen," she mused and flipped the photograph over. "Is this your picture, Clarisse?" she asked curiously.

"It was left here by a ruggedly handsome man called Searcy. As you can probably tell by the name, he's a pig."

"A cop?" Trudy asked, and looked harder at the picture.

"It's a morgue shot, Trudy. That's why it looks so strange," said Clarisse. Valentine was at the other end of the bar.

Trudy's thickly lashed eyes fluttered up. "Morgue...?" she asked hesitantly.

Clarisse nodded and pulled the newspaper around so Trudy could see the headline. "That's the little boy who embarrassed Scarpetti."

Trudy turned the print facedown again. "I heard on the radio," she muttered. "Hustlers are such sweet little boys. Who'd want to kill a sweet little boy?"

"That's what this cop Searcy wanted to find out. He was in here just a little while ago asking questions."

"What kind of questions?"

"You know, was the kid ever in here or not. That sort of thing."

"The boy was never in here," said Trudy firmly.

"That's what Valentine told the man."

Valentine returned with another drink for Trudy. She downed a swift swallow. "The police follow trouble, the police cause trouble. It's all so upsetting. I haven't been touched by a cop since '59. Five of 'em marched in here on Valentine's Day and arrested me for impersonating Doris Duke."

Valentine smiled. "You don't look a thing like Doris Duke. Of course, I've only seen pictures of her."

"The police thought there was a great similarity. Maybe there had been complaints. We do both have tasteful wardrobes, and in '59 it was illegal to impersonate Doris on the street." Trudy sighed. "Well," she said, "time to see how many hearts I can break. It's a 'Send in the Clowns' night. Can I have the newspaper to read on my break, Valentine?"

He nodded and she folded the paper under her arm. After greeting several of her admirers, she sat at the lacquered piano and played the promised song.

Clarisse turned to Valentine and found him staring blankly toward the foyer. She touched his hand that rested on the bar. "When are you going to call Searcy?" she asked.

Chapter Five

LIEUTENANT WILLIAM Searcy was angry with himself when he left Bonaparte's. He had entered as a cop, with authority and with purpose, but everyone there had seemed to get the better of him: the bartender Valentine, the woman Clarisse in her fur coat, even the hatcheck woman who wouldn't look at him. He returned to his car, which was parked beside a fire hydrant, and sat inside it until the heater had warmed him.

Searcy rested back heavily in the seat. He lit a cigarette, drew the smoke deeply into his throat, and released it slowly as he rubbed his eyes. He was grateful that only half an hour more of duty remained tonight.

Searcy was thirty-six, and his life had been such that he showed every day of his age. After a short and uneventful tour of Vietnam, he had joined the Chicago police force, where his record in undercover vice work had been outstanding. As his superior infelicitously wrote in his record, "Searcy has an affinity for vice." Though he had grown up on the South Side of Chicago, and his mother lived there still, Searcy had not been reluctant to leave the city when the opportunity arose. That chance was a temporary transfer to Boston, as a consultant to the vice squad there. When a large promotion was offered as a bribe to stay on, Searcy unhesitatingly accepted.

He had been in Boston six years now, but gradually was working his way out of vice. Most of his time now was spent in investigating petty larceny and murders that didn't want much investigating. He rarely communicated with his mother, whom he didn't like; his father was long since dead; and his younger sister was living in San Luis Obispo the last he had heard, but doing what, he had no idea—and didn't care. When Searcy was put to the extremity of enumerating his friends, he named the two men with whom he played squash each week, but neither of these men did he really like, and of them he knew little more than that they too were policemen.

When he had finished his cigarette, Searcy drove off, headed down the three short anonymous blocks that separated the essentially residential Bay Village from the essentially urban Park Square.

Park Square is the half-respectable suburb of the Combat Zone where, directly across from the Teddybear Lounge, with its orange and purple neon, and its flyblown montage of semi-nude strippers with exotic names and hardened faces, stands the eminently fashionable Park Plaza Hotel. Lincolns and Cadillacs line the block here to pick up and drop off hotel residents. At one end of Park Square is the Greyhound terminal and at the other end the Trailways. On the third side is Hillbilly Heaven, a country music bar with a perennial floorshow of fistfights, and on the fourth is Shreve, Crump & Lowe, one of the most prestigious jewelers in America, older than Tiffany's.

Park Square is hustlers' turf.

Searcy circled about and came into the square from the south. Inside the glass double doors of Trailways a lone female passenger struggled with two large suitcases done up with thick rope. Under the awning of the Seamen's Grill, next to the terminal, a skinny weary whore shivered beneath green neon.

He twice circled the statue commemorating the Emancipation Proclamation, and moved up between the

Teddybear Lounge and the Park Plaza. He drew up into a legiti-
mate parking space, turned the heat on high, and lit another
cigarette.

When he had finished the cigarette, he lowered the
window to let the stale hot air out of the car. The fresh air
braced him, and he felt motivated to drive on, across Arlington
Street, and slowly past the Greyhound terminal. Evidently a bus
had just come in, and considering the number of persons hailing
cabs, he judged that it was from New York. He double-parked
directly across from the terminal, stretched across the seat, and
stared up and down the dark sidewalk.

It wasn't really surprising that one day after a murder the
street would be clear, and yet he had expected at least one
young man to be slouched in a shallow doorway, or leaning
against the cold wet concrete, or making some pretense of
hitching. There was no one.

Searcy drove to the corner of Berkeley Street, turned
right, and immediately made another right onto Providence
Street. Providence Street had the unsavory but accurate nickname of Vaseline Alley. It was a narrow dark passageway with
large garbage bins piled up under the dim red lights of delivery
entrances. Searcy drove slowly. An old Rambler with a flat
tire was run up over the curb, a dark glass beer bottle stood
upright in the middle of the street, but he could see no one. No
shadowy figure ducked behind a barrel, no little groups turned
to hide their lighted joints, there was not even a drunk taking
a piss. The hustlers, fearing either the cold or the murder, had
evidently taken refuge in the bars.

Searcy eased out onto lighted Arlington Street, and by
going the wrong way up a one-way street and making a U-turn,
he found another parking space. For the walk to Nexus, a couple
of blocks away, he lit another cigarette. He passed through the
Trailways lot, slapped at the side of a bus to see how cold the
metal was, and then turned onto Carver Street, which was
shorter, darker, and narrower than Vaseline Alley.

In the middle of this short cobbled passage between tall

unlighted brick buildings is an incongruous Spanish facade in white stucco and iron grillwork; the building houses a restaurant called by its address, where no one has ever eaten, and Herbie's Ramrod Room, a gay denim-and-leather bar, that is as venerable and as pleasant as Bonaparte's but not nearly so respectable.

As Searcy passed on the narrow sidewalk, two tall rangy bearded men wearing enough black leather to shoe the entire Boston police force stepped out of Herbie's vestibule, blocking Searcy's path. They were laughing, but broke off when they saw him; both looked him steadily up and down.

"Get rid of the suit," said the taller sternly to Searcy. "It doesn't do a thing for you."

"I got a pair of jeans and a jock in my trunk that ought to fit you fine," said the shorter. "Come try 'em on."

They maintained their cocky but not unfriendly stare.

Searcy said nothing. He was reaching inside his jacket to pull out his police identification, but the two men inched apart just enough to let him pass through if he wished.

When he turned onto Boylston Street, Searcy heard their laughter again behind him. He hurried angrily into Nexus.

Just inside the entrance to the bar, Searcy hand-combed his curly hair and straightened his jacket. He pulled off his tie and slipped it folded into his back pocket.

The music from the dance floor at the bottom of the ramp was unidentifiable, but the beat was unmistakably disco. About seventy-five dancers were on the floor, twice as many men as women. The tables along the walls were occupied by excited old men trying to talk above the music, and bored young men who pretended that they couldn't hear a word.

Searcy edged along the dance floor and took a stool at the end of the bar, deliberately removed from the middle-aged bartender in yellow suspenders who was busy at the other end with dancers between their feverish bouts with the music. From this quietest corner of Nexus, Searcy began a methodical examination of everyone in the cavernous room. His first subject was not what he had expected to find in the town's principal bar for hustlers. A young woman, only a few seats down from him, was unaccountably dressed as Daisy Mae Yokum; her abbreviated costume was hardly enough to protect her from the gusts of frigid air that bellowed down the great ramp each time the outside door was opened. Daisy Mae had finger scratches down her left thigh and a set of TWA stewardess wings pinned over a nipple. She leaned back against the bar, bare legs crossed high, stirring a drink with a long-nailed finger, and staring about her with singular contentment.

"Can I help you?"

Searcy looked up at the bartender and shook his head, but said nothing.

"Do you want a drink or not? I'm probably not going to be back up in this neck of the woods for a good ten minutes."

Searcy stared at him for a moment. "I'll be off duty by then." He reached inside his coat pocket, but the bartender placed a hand lightly on Searcy's arm.

"Don't show me. You reach like a cop—I believe you. You pull that thing out, and there's a stampede up that ramp in about ten seconds. And I want my tips tonight. We've got a good crowd for Tuesday."

Searcy nodded, and introduced himself.

"My name's Mack," said the bartender. "The clock behind the bar is wrong. You're off duty now. What'll you have?"

"Bourbon and water."

Mack turned to the bar and mixed the drink. Moving back, he motioned to a waiter standing nearby. The young man crossed behind the bar, and began waiting on the dancers. Mack slid the glass across to Searcy and then came around himself. He placed himself as a shield between Searcy and the rest of the room.

"You're here about Billy Golacinsky, right?" Mack said.

Searcy pulled another morgue photo from his pocket and handed it to the bartender. "The one and only." Mack studied it for a moment and shook his head.

"Well, what do you want to know?"

"When did you see him last?"

"Last night."

Searcy took a slow swallow of his drink, studying the man. "What was he doing here?"

"What everybody else comes to Nexus for—get plastered, dance their ass off, you know—have a good time." Mack shrugged.

Searcy put his glass down. "Come on, Mack, I'm not from Rhode Island. This is a hustler bar and everybody knows it. I told you, or you said it—I came in here about Billy Golacinsky. I'm not interested in little boys, no matter how old they are, and I'm not interested in old men who *are* interested in little boys. Let 'em keep each other company. But I *am* interested in Billy Golacinsky, because he's dead. Now, you can talk to me over this bourbon or you can talk to me across the top of my desk at nine o'clock tomorrow morning."

"Wait a minute, Lieutenant, you just didn't let me get started. Once I get started, you can't shut me up, but I got to ease into it, that's all."

"Sorry," said Searcy grudgingly. "But I've been out all day looking for somebody who saw him, and you're the first one. You had seen him before last night, I take it. You're the first one who's called him Billy."

"Billy came in here four times a week, at least. He was still new in town, said he came from California, but he didn't even know that San Francisco was north of L.A. Anyway, that's the kind he was, the kind who would lie about something like that because he thought that being from California, he could charge a higher price. Not very smart."

"What about last night?"

"He got here about this time. His hair was wet from the snow and he looked awful, so he sat down, on the same stool you're on, and dried off and warmed up. I was watching him, I felt a little sorry for him. I feel a little sorry for all of 'em. He was in a bad way. He couldn't decide whether he was cold or drunk or horny or poor or all of 'em put together. But he was definitely in here to get picked up."

"Did you see him talking to anyone?"

"Sort of."

"What does that mean?"

"Well, there was this older guy who started sending beers over to the kid. Got him pretty drunk before he went over to him. Cheap trick, but it works like gold."

"Who was this guy? The one buying the drinks?"

"Never saw him before."

"Well then, what did he look like?"

Mack turned halfway on the stool, and discreetly pointed across the room at the line of tables. "See that man? He looked like him."

"Which one?" demanded Searcy. "Which one are you pointing at?"

"I'm pointing at all of 'em," said Mack. "They're all after the same thing. They all have the same expression. And they all look alike."

"Yeah, but you said he was buying beers from you for Golacinsky. He must have come up to the bar a few times."

"He was short," said Mack, "and he had white hair, or gray hair maybe. I'm not sure. It wasn't dyed. Clean shaven."

Searcy sighed. "What was he wearing?"

"A dark overcoat. He never checked it."

"What color?"

"Black. Brown. Dark green. How can you tell under these lights? A double-knit leisure suit. It looked like it had come off the rack about an hour before, that big place on the South Shore that advertises on Channel 56. He looked South Shore, deep South Shore. Sharon maybe, or Randolph."

Searcy glared at Mack suspiciously. "You talked to him, didn't you?"

Mack shook his head. "It's just a feeling."

"Did they leave together?"

"I'm not sure. But I would say yes, if I had to. Daisy Mae behind me here had a little action going in the middle of the dance floor, and I had to play bouncer for a while. After I had treated the claw marks, Billy was gone, and so was the leisure suit from Sharon."

"Well, let me ask you this," said Searcy with growing impatience, "you think it's possible that this 'leisure suit from Sharon' might have..."

"Killed Billy? You mean, did he look like violence?"

Searcy nodded.

"No," said Mack flatly, "not the type. And let me tell you something, Lieutenant: I know the type."

"Yeah?"

"I did time."

Searcy took a deep breath and lit a cigarette. "What else about the kid?"

"Not much. He didn't talk a lot. Hustlers don't, in general. Sometimes Billy made money, sometimes he didn't. You could tell when he had money, because he'd always pay with the biggest bill that he had in his pocket. He'd turn a trick and come in here with a couple of twenties. If he came in here and paid with a dollar, I'd know he didn't have much left."

"What'd he have last night?"

"I didn't charge him. Holiday spirit, and all. Billy was a runaway. If he had been smarter, he would have been lonely and unhappy. But he had his little dreams too, just like the rest of us."

"You knew him pretty well."

Mack shook his head, a little sadly. "No. I hear a lot, and I see these people every day. And there's not much to see. As I say, they don't talk much, but when they do it's right to the point. Sometime before Thanksgiving Billy was in here one night, and he sat down and ordered a Miller's—that's what he drank, always. He was sitting there, smoothing out a whole wad of dollar bills. He told me he was saving his money now for a face job."

"A nineteen-year-old hustler was saving up to have a face-lift?"

Mack laughed. "No, a face job. He had mottled skin, you can see it here in the picture." Mack pointed to the photograph.

"He was going to get a peel or something so his face would look like a baby's ass, all smooth and all. Said it would increase his business."

Searcy shook his head and laughed. "What did you say when he told you that?"

"Oh, I told him great, that he should do it if he wanted it."

Searcy was silent for a moment. He checked his watch. "Right now," he said, "my own little dream has come true. I'm officially off duty, by my watch. Another bourbon, but straight up. I'll pay you with the biggest bill I've got."

Mack laughed, slipped off the stool, and went around behind the bar. In passing, he tickled Daisy Mae's ribs. She laughed shrilly, and swiveled to face Searcy.

Her attempt at a shy smile was so bizarre that Searcy was hard put not to laugh aloud.

"Hi," she said, in a not very good southern accent, "nice night, hunh? I saw you come in. You came in all by yourself, but what I want to know is, are you planning to go out the same way?"

Searcy smiled. "Payday's tomorrow. Tonight I'm broke."

Daisy Mae closed her disbelieving eyes. She opened them and sighed. "Well then, don't let me waste your time." She shook her thick ponytails, and straightened up. She looked back at him. "Listen, honey, if you're looking for a piece of free chicken, you came to the wrong place. The boys in here have dollar signs tattooed all over their precious little bodies."

"I'm not interested in that either."

"Listen, on account of its being cold and you being so good-looking, I think I could manage a full ten-dollar discount."

Mack stood between them, on the other side of the bar.

"Thanks," said Searcy, "not tonight."

Daisy Mae gulped her drink. "Honestly, Mack, you think it would do any good if I laid myself at his feet? Some nights you can't even give it away."

"I know," said Mack sympathetically. From beneath the bar Mack produced a voluminous waist-length rabbit coat. Daisy stood and pulled it on. She closed the bottom button and took a deep breath, which lifted her breasts high. She raised her hand and wiggled it at Mack. "I'm off to find somebody who needs a bit of five-finger exercise to get his blood going again. Listen, honey," she said, turning to Searcy, "you change your mind, you'll find me at the end of Carver, frozen to the bricks."

She headed for the exit. Her walk was between a trot and a bounce. She hit the ramp and disappeared.

"I think she was interested in you," said Mack.

Searcy laughed, a little uneasily.

"I'm glad you didn't give her any grief, being a cop and all, I mean."

"I'm not the vice," said Searcy.

"Listen, I got to get back, Lieutenant. I'm missing my tips. Anything else you want to know?"

"I want you to think hard about this older man, what he looked like, exactly what he looked like. You *could* be wrong about the South Shore. I'll call you tomorrow, day after, and if you've got anything, I'll have you in to make up a composite."

Mack was silent for a moment. "There was something else."

"What?"

"Billy sometimes took his tricks to the baths. Maybe that's where they went after they left here. Maybe Billy made the man take him to the baths."

"Why would he do that?"

"Because he got the best deal that way. The john would pay for the room. They'd have sex, and the john would pay Billy and go home. Billy had a place to stay for the night and all the free sex he wanted. He made out both ways. It's a smart idea—probably not his. Maybe you ought to check the baths."

"Any particular one?"

Mack rubbed his chin. "Only two in town. But Billy went to the Royal Baths, I think." He looked at Searcy. "I'm not really sure."

Searcy stood to go. He was surprised when Mack stuck his hand across the bar to be shaken.

Searcy shook his hand and said, "Listen, you're not one of them, are you?" He cocked his head toward the dance floor. "You're not a fag."

Mack paused before answering. "No," he replied quietly.

"Then why do you work in this place, why do you hang out with these people?"

Mack dropped Searcy's hand, and picked up a towel. "I tell you, Lieutenant: twenty-five years ago, it was straight men that got me in trouble, and ten years ago, it was straight men that got me put in jail. It was a *fag* that got me out of jail, and it was a *fag* that made sure I got a decent job. I got *nothing* against 'em. I'm not a fag, but I know what they know"—he gestured just as Searcy had, with a cocked head—"that straight men are just trouble."

Searcy turned to go, but Mack arrested him in a friendlier voice: "Listen, Lieutenant, Daisy Mae's turning blue. Tonight, I don't think she'd charge a thing."

Wednesday, 3 January

Chapter Six

As DANIEL VALENTINE roused himself from sleep, a fine mist of snow was falling from a sky of low-hung, steel-gray clouds.

With a practiced, sure motion he swept the alarm clock from the bedside table onto the floor, seconds before the alarm was to sound. It landed on the alarm button and the clock never rang.

Valentine opened his eye not buried in the pillow, and noted the snow with some satisfaction. He raised one arm and brought it firmly down onto the pillow behind him.

No one was there.

Valentine opened his eyes and turned over. He had the feeling that someone ought to have been lying on the other half of the bed, although he had no idea who.

He stared across the shadowed room to the bath. The door was ajar, and he could see that it was empty.

Valentine shrugged and pushed back the covers. He swung his legs over onto the chill floor, and quickly raised them again. He coughed to see how cold the air in his lungs was, and finding it very cold, he rubbed his arms violently for warmth.

He stared at the other half of the bed, looking for proof of someone's having slept there. He saw none; perhaps it had been only a dream.

Taking a deep breath he padded across the cold hardwood floor to the bathroom. A long shower warmed him but didn't do much toward waking him up. He pulled on a red flannel shirt, worn jeans, and heavy white wool athletic socks.

Crossing the hallway toward the living room, he flicked the thermostat up to 70. Beyond the living room was the small kitchen, much too narrow for the red deal table he had placed in it. While water heated for instant coffee, he stood at the window and stared out at Fayette Street three floors below. His single thought was that the irregular spitting of snow was not going to block the streets; he would, in all good conscience, have to go to the health club in the afternoon.

After he had stared awhile into the empty street, he stared at the three Boston ferns that hung in the kitchen window. Their fronds were tipped with yellow; they needed to be thinned and cut back. He couldn't remember when he'd watered them last. The ferns were a gift from Clarisse, who had had a short affair with a wholesale florist. Valentine decided that it would actually be more cruel to water them than not, thereby drawing out their inevitable death by dehydration and neglect.

Valentine pressed a finger into the soil of one of the pots. To his surprise it was moist; Clarisse had evidently been watering them behind his back.

To counteract her care of the plants, he opened the window a couple of inches, from the top, so that the cold air would blow in on the ferns. He had never been able to explain to his friends that he resented the demands put upon him by green plants—there was something continually reproachful in their complete helplessness.

He much preferred the notion of the Christmas tree. You bring in a fine plant that, without any attention being paid it, remains perfectly beautiful for three weeks. Then it is thrown out, or burnt in the fireplace, and never thought of again. Valentine complacently looked at his own Christmas tree, which he had decorated with three very fine packs of late-nineteenth-century Austrian playing cards. He had ingeniously constructed a web of invisible nylon thread to hold the cards in place about the tree, for it would have been unthinkable to drill holes in the cards, which had been an important and expensive addition to his collection.

Clarisse had groaned when she saw the tree, for there were times that she considered his collecting an obsession. He had his finest cards set in large frames and placed on all the walls of the rooms in his flat, and had playing cards embedded beneath the glass of the coffee table. Kitchen drawers, drawers in the bedside table and living room end tables, were filled with uncatalogued packs, there were albums and boxes of cards stacked high in the corners of the bedroom. Clarisse once suggested that he take down some of the cards and put up pictures of naked men, since so many playing cards made her think of Las Vegas; so Valentine replaced a pack that he had grown tired of with one that pictured a naked man on each card. When she saw this, Clarisse had sighed and given up. "It would be different if you liked to play poker, or bridge, or—"

"I hate card games," Valentine had said.

The kettle whistled. He poured the boiling water into a cup that held three times the recommended amount of instant coffee, and took the mug into the living room. He sat on the overstuffed white sofa that faced the bay window. He smiled to see the snow falling more heavily.

He had raised the cup to his lips, when he noticed a neatly folded piece of blue notepaper resting above the jack of clubs embedded in the coffee table. He put the coffee down, picked the note up, unfolded and read it. In neat clear script was written: *"Had to get to work early. Didn't want to wake you. Thanks for a great time. Call me soon. Your number wasn't on the phone, so I'll just leave mine."* It gave the telephone number, a Boston exchange, and was signed *"Gary."*

It had been no dream. Valentine tried to remember what Gary looked like.

Valentine raised the cup to his lips, and the door buzzer sounded. He groaned, and swallowed a quarter of the cup of burning coffee. On the fifth insistent buzz, he went to the door and pressed the intercom.

It was Clarisse's voice, quick and blurred. After thirty seconds of incomprehensible speech, Valentine pressed the door-release button for a sarcastically long time, opened the door, and retreated to the sofa.

A few moments later, Clarisse rushed in. She was wearing her fur coat, but no hat. As Valentine watched, droplets of snow melted in her thick black hair like tiny dissolving pearls. Under one arm was her leather envelope with a newspaper sticking out of it, and in her other hand was a glazed paper bag, torn, with the logo of an expensive and fashionable Italian bakery on it.

"Gorgeous day!" she cried, and kicked the door shut. She threw the envelope and the bag onto the glass table, and then pulled off her coat. Beneath she wore full-cut black corduroy slacks and a white silk blouse opened one button too many. Around her neck was a gold chain fashioned of square links.

The coat flew over Valentine's head and fell behind the couch.

"It's too early in the morning for June Allyson," said Valentine sulkily.

"No," said Clarisse, "I'm Faye Dunaway this morning. To do June Allyson, I'd have to be drunk." She craned her neck in several directions. "Where is he?" she demanded.

"Who?"

"The man of the hour. The trick of the day?"

"He left. I was too much for him."

"Too bad," she said, disappointed. "I brought breakfast for three." She ran to the kitchen, leaned through the doorframe, balancing precariously on one high-heeled shoe, and flicked on the flame under the water.

"Why are you out so early?"

"Guilt," replied Clarisse, turning back with a ravishing smile. "This morning I got up and decided I was going to pull a real nine-to-fiver. First one in, last one out. That office wouldn't know what hit it."

Valentine glanced at the clock on the mantel. "You mean you already put in two hours?"

Clarisse paused. "Actually, no," she admitted. "I haven't quite made it in yet. I left the apartment though at eight-thirty. I really did. But it was so cold I couldn't put in my contacts, because I was afraid they'd freeze to my pupils, and I got on the wrong train, and I ended up at Haymarket. So as long as I was there, I figured I might as well have coffee with this cute fireman who was just getting off duty, and I did, and we have a date, and you'll be real jealous if I ever let you meet him, and then I thought that as long as I was *still* there, I might as well run across to the North End and buy you and Mr. Nameless some breakfast, and then I was headed back and I remembered that my passport needed to be renewed so I stopped in at Government Center and filled out all the forms, and ran across the street to have my picture taken, and here I am. I'm considering this an early lunch hour."

"I don't know why you even try."

"Well," said Clarisse, returning languidly to the kitchen to prepare coffee for herself, "I feel so virtuous, you just can't imagine."

Valentine had pulled the newspaper out of her leather envelope and opened it onto his lap.

"It's on page three, lower right," called Clarisse from the kitchen.

A small headline above a short column read, NEW CLUE IN HUSTLER DEATH. Valentine read the first sentence, lost the sense of it, and brushed the newspaper off his lap onto the floor.

"Not ready for the gory details this early?" said Clarisse.

"Not awake."

"Then don't read the Letters to the Editor either. Some imbecilic woman from Jamaica Plain wrote in, talking about Billy G., saying he was one down and seventy-five thousand to go—"

"Not a bad estimate for a bigot," remarked Valentine. "That is, if she was talking about just Boston."

"—and that she thought it was a good sign that he had been dumped on Scarpetti's lawn, except that his grass probably wouldn't ever grow there again, and that she hoped someone was seeing to it that the boy wasn't buried in consecrated ground."

"That's great. Find out her address, and later we'll ride by and fire-bomb her house. That'll be one bigot down, and two hundred million to go."

Clarisse tossed the bakery bag into Valentine's lap. He opened it, handed Clarisse an enormous sweet bun filled with honey and covered with crushed walnuts. He took a second one out for himself.

"This snow could get on my nerves if it keeps up," said Clarisse. "Maybe you and I ought to go away somewhere."

"Sure," said Valentine, "let's go back to Bermuda. We can stay in that hotel where we met—relive our first happy days together—"

"Yes," said Clarisse. "Those happy days when I fell in love with you by the pool, those happy nights in my cabana, and those happy mornings that you spent in bed with the assistant manager—"

"I didn't know quite how to break it to you..."

"I thought your impotence was *my* fault—but by the time you got around to me in the evening, you were just worn out. God was I upset when I found out!"

"I would have been impotent *without* the assistant manager," smiled Valentine, consolingly.

"So why did you even try?"

"Because you were in love with me, and I was in love with your tits. I still am."

"Let's go to Rio instead," said Clarisse. "Rio's great this time of year."

"I can't afford Rio," said Valentine.

"You could if you didn't spend half your salary on a maid for this three-room apartment."

"I have to have someone to clean. Housecleaning depresses me. That's something else that makes me impotent. I don't even like to watch other people cleaning. That's why Joyce comes in at night, when I'm at Bonaparte's."

"You've got the only maid in town who comes in three times a week to watch the late movie!"

"Clarisse, I'm not paying her for the work she does, but for the work that I don't have to do."

"Anyway, if you weren't supporting Joyce and her two husbands, you'd have enough money to go to Rio."

"Probably." Valentine shrugged.

They finished the buns in silence, watching the snow blowing against the bay window.

Clarisse pushed the last bit of pastry into her mouth, licked her fingers, and sat up. "Nearly forgot. Guess who called this morning?"

From the tone of her voice he knew. He closed his eyes, dropped his head against the back of the sofa, and groaned. He lifted his head, opened his eyes, and said, "Mark."

"He called at seven-thirty. Seven-thirty in the morning, can you imagine? To chat?!"

"Clarisse, he works at a logging camp. He was probably already on his second morning coffee break. Why did he call?"

"Because your number is unlisted. He fell in love with you and you wouldn't even give him your phone number."

"Only two people in the world have my phone number. You and my father."

"Why are you so mean to Mark?"

"I'm not mean to him."

"Yes you are. All he wants is to see you once in a while. It must be lonely up there in the wilds of New Hampshire—"

"—surrounded by three hundred lumberjacks—"

"Yes," said Clarisse, "but he's not in love with them, he's in love with you."

"Clarisse," said Valentine, with hard-got patience, "he stayed here two weeks last summer. If you're generous, I suppose you could call that an affair. It began in August, it ended in August. How can you take seriously anything that begins and ends in August? Hot nights and steamy days for two weeks, and then he asks me to marry him. I could have accepted I suppose, but my heart wouldn't have been in it. Mark is hot, Mark has the body of death, Mark is just about the handsomest most rugged man I've ever come across in my life, and he'll make somebody a great wife, but not me!"

Clarisse smiled condescendingly. "He'll be here tomorrow to renew the proposal."

"What?!"

"I promised him I wouldn't tell you. He wanted to surprise you. I swore on my mother's grave I wouldn't tell you."

"Your mother's not dead."

"She's got her plot. Anyway, he said he'd be in about dinnertime."

"How can I get away from him?"

"We could go to Ibiza," suggested Clarisse. "He wouldn't find us on Ibiza."

"Call him back," said Valentine, "tell him I have infectious hepatitis. Tell him—"

"Eat the third roll," said Clarisse, "you'll feel better if you're fat."

Valentine tore open the bag and devoured the pastry.

Neither said anything for a few moments.

Clarisse pointed to the discarded newspaper. "Don't you want to know what the new clue is?"

"No."

"It's a lipstick smear."

Valentine looked up. He brushed sugar and crushed walnuts from his moustache and beard. "That kid wasn't the type, not even for clear gloss."

"It wasn't on him. It was on a handkerchief."

"And?"

Clarisse looked at him blankly. "That's all. It was in his back pocket."

"And?" Valentine demanded again.

"Maybe Billy was with a woman that night. Maybe a woman killed him and then kissed him in the handkerchief."

"Maybe," said Valentine doubtfully. "Maybe she could have bashed his head in with a single blow, but she'd have to have been built like Catherine the Great."

"Billy was just a scrawny kid, so maybe it was just a lucky hit. Or maybe it was teamwork—a man *and* a woman."

Valentine crumpled the bakery bag. "What are you getting at?"

"Maybe Searcy is looking in the wrong place. The dead kid was a hustler and so the police are looking for a gay killer. But maybe, if it was a woman..."

Valentine stood and walked to the bay window. He stared at the snow. He turned and stared at Clarisse. "Maybe a hooker kissed his handkerchief. Maybe he lent it to a drag queen in the bus station. If the police had thought it was an important clue, they wouldn't have released it to the press."

"Maybe it was leaked, maybe the police didn't want the information to get out. The *Globe's* against Scarpetti, and they'd probably like to see it turn out that this kid was murdered by a straight couple out for sleazy thrills."

"That's a bit involved for the *Globe*, don't you think? They have enough trouble deciding whether they're for or against fresh water."

"Have you talked to that good-looking cop yet?"

"Searcy?"

Clarisse nodded.

"I called. He wasn't there. I left a message."

"You're making excuses, Val, you—"

The telephone rang.

"Must be your father," said Clarisse, "*I'm* already here."

"I gave my number to the cop to call back." Valentine picked up the receiver.

It was Searcy. "I got your message just this minute, I—"

Valentine heard two telephones ring on Searcy's end.

"Just a minute," said Searcy. The line went blank.

Valentine sighed and leaned against the cold glass of the bay window. "I love it. First man I've given my number to in two years, and he puts me on hold."

Clarisse leaned forward over the coffee table. She had taken a small plastic contact-lens holder and a bottle of wetting solution from her leather envelope, and was snapping the lenses into her eyes. The left one went in immediately, but the second popped off her finger into the high pile of the carpet.

"Hang up, hang up!" she shrieked.

"What the hell's going on?" Searcy demanded. Valentine had not heard the line reconnect.

"That was Clarisse," said Valentine.

She had dropped to her hands and knees on the carpet.

"Who?" said Searcy.

"The woman in Bonaparte's."

There was a pause. "In the checkroom...?"

"That's Irene. Clarisse, the one with the big—"

One cheek against the carpet, Clarisse glared at Valentine.

"—big fur coat," said Valentine.

"I remember," said Searcy.

Valentine gave Searcy a circumstantial account of meeting Golacinsky on the Block.

"Well," said Searcy, "I'm glad you decided to come clean—"

"What!"

"You're sure you didn't take Golacinsky back to your place for a quickie? You could have afforded what a kid like that was charging. He wasn't—"

"Lieutenant, I told you what happened." Valentine gripped the receiver hard. "There was nothing else."

"Well," said Searcy then, "it won't do me much good. I was hoping that you had called about something important. I've talked to a number of people already who saw him after you ran into him on the Block. What you've given me isn't much help."

"You told me to call if I had *any* information."

Searcy, ignoring the apparent anger in Valentine's voice, said, "Did you show that picture around?"

"Yes."

"Anything?"

"No."

"Nobody recognized the photograph?"

"Of course not. I told you, we don't let that kind of cheap hustler in."

"You found him quick enough on the Block," said Searcy coldly, "but the next—"

Valentine didn't hear the request. He had dropped the receiver softly in its cradle.

Chapter Seven

IT WAS THE LAST quarter hour of a beautiful cold dusk when Searcy pulled up in front of Professor Lawrence's house. He hurried up the sidewalk and stood on the front porch; a frigid wind swept out of the luminous blue sky and froze all five fingers as he pushed the doorbell.

He looked through the leaded-glass panels beside the wide oaken door, and saw that the rooms in the rear of the house were softly and warmly lighted. Waiting, he pulled his collar high up on his neck, and turned toward the Scarpetti house, large and iridescently white beneath black trees. The snow in the yard was dirty and trampled, and the dead lawn had been whipped up into frozen waves of mud near the sidewalk.

A coupe of locks were slid back. Searcy turned to the door as it was pulled open.

Professor Lawrence was evidently not pleased to receive a caller. Though his eyes were politely blank, his mouth was set in an irritated crease. He wore a carefully ironed green flannel shirt, carefully pressed brown trousers, and shiny brown leather slippers. Over this was a large white chef's apron, the breast of which was smeared with blood.

"Professor Lawrence?" Searcy asked.

Lawrence nodded. "Are you a reporter?" he asked.

Searcy reached inside his coat and pulled out his wallet. When he flipped it open, the plastic crackled in the cold. "I'm not going to ruin my eyes trying to read in this light. Are you the police?"

Searcy introduced himself. Lawrence smiled for the first time. "That's very clever," he said.

"What?" demanded Searcy.

"The name. Circe. Patroness of Pigs."

Searcy cringed. "It's S-E-A-R-C-Y."

"Pity," said Lawrence. "Well, please come inside. My apron's getting stiff in the cold. What can I do for you?" They moved into a long hallway, wood-paneled and lighted from above in dim yellow. The floor was soft with thick Oriental runners.

"I'm sorry to be bothering you now, but I was wondering if you might answer some questions?"

"Two men came over and ruined my morning, I typed out a statement myself, I signed it in triplicate. It had down everything I know about what happened, and my little part in the drama. What more is there?"

Searcy seemed embarrassed. "I—I, ummn…haven't seen your statement…"

Lawrence said, wearily, "Come in back, then."

They moved past the darkened living room into the dining room, where a hardwood fire burned evenly in the hearth. The warm light was caught and flashed off the heavy crystal glassware on a formal table set for six.

Lawrence passed through this room into a narrow L-shaped kitchen. He picked up a Chinese cleaver and continued to slice thinly a large slab of pinkish-brown meat on a thick cutting board. Searcy stood in front of the fireplace, warming his hands behind him. He could see the professor easily, and so did not move nearer the kitchen.

"Would you like a drink, Lieutenant Searcy? It's still a good name," he added, apparently to himself, "even if it's spelled differently."

Searcy hesitated. "Coffee, if you have it."

"With cognac?" Without waiting for a reply, Lawrence disappeared around the bend in the L. Searcy removed his overcoat, and laid it carefully over the back of a chair. He turned down his collar, and rubbed his hands gratefully in the warmth of the fire.

He glanced back toward the kitchen and started. At the cutting board stood a Chinese boy, no more than twenty-one, who had silently taken up the chore of slicing the meat. His black hair was worn fairly long, and shone almost blue. He wore black pants and a black sweater, and his blue-veined feet were shod in thick black sandals with black velvet straps and woven grass tops. He did not look at Searcy.

Lawrence came around the corner of the L again, carrying two large cups of coffee. He stood at the threshold to the kitchen. The Chinese boy carefully wiped the cleaver and disappeared.

"Here you are."

Searcy crossed and took the cup from Lawrence, who returned to the cutting board, and sipped from his cup as they talked. Searcy leaned in the doorway.

"I didn't know that a professor's salary could afford a houseboy," said Searcy casually.

"Houseboy?"

"The Chinese kid."

"Oh. Neville's not a houseboy. He lives here, with me."

Searcy swallowed hard. "Oh, I'm sorry...Jesus Christ, isn't anybody straight anymore?"

Lawrence raised the cleaver high. "In Boston?" He brought the cleaver down and neatly halved a morsel of meat. "Well, there's Scarpetti, who claims to be straight. That's one. Are you straight?"

"Yes," said Searcy.

"So, that's two," said Lawrence. He scooped up the meat and dropped it into a shining steel bowl. He lifted the cutting board and held it out beside him. Neville suddenly was there to take it to the sink. "Have you scraped the ginger?" Lawrence asked.

Neville nodded once, said nothing, did not look up from the sink.

"Now, Lieutenant," said Lawrence, "I know you have a job, and a murder to solve, and a state representative to exonerate, but I have a dinner party for six, and I haven't even salted my ducks. So, if you don't mind, could we get on with it?" He took the cutting board from Neville, and set it back on the counter. Neville then handed him two long stalks of pale green vegetables, that looked to be a cross between celery and lettuce, and which Searcy was sure he had never eaten or even seen before. Deftly, with the cleaver, Lawrence began to chop them to shreds.

"That night," said Searcy, after another swallow of the coffee, "did you hear anything at all outside? You know, loud voices, a car, anything?"

"You know, the Boston police have a reputation for efficiency, but maybe that's only in months that don't have an *r* in them. Why didn't your superior let you see my statement before you drove out here?"

"My superior didn't send me here. I came on my own."

"How aggressive of you. All right, though."

Lawrence set aside the cleaver and wiped his hands on a part of the apron not stained with blood. He picked up his coffee and crossed past Searcy into the dining room. On either side of the fireplace stood a carved high-backed armchair. Lawrence settled himself into one and motioned for Searcy to take the other. He did. The firelight played off their faces as they looked at one another across the bright hot hearth.

"Now, Lieutenant Searcy, I'm going to do for you what I don't do for anybody: I'm going to repeat myself, tell you what I told your friends in the force this morning. But that will be it." He smiled blandly.

"I understand," said Searcy.

"Nothing," said Lawrence, "I heard nothing that night. No car prowling through the predawn hours, no voices raised in anger, no sickening thud, no car doors slamming. I slept well that night, and dreamt of Coney Island. When I went out that morning, there was only one set of tire tracks in the snow. It came up to the hemlocks, and then repeated itself going back down toward Route 60."

"You must have thought that was strange if you noticed it…"

"I notice everything," said Lawrence. "I assumed that someone belonging to the Scarpettis had parked there for a while. Scarpetti often has ill-dressed men visit him in the middle of the night."

"What about the car door opening and closing?" Searcy said.

"Someone trying to dispose of a dead teenager is not going to slam all four doors going about it. At night anyway, this is a quiet neighborhood. I would have heard it if it had been at all loud."

"Are your storm windows up?"

"Not in the bedroom. I believe in fresh air. I would have heard," he said again.

"You were in all evening?"

Lawrence nodded. "Neville and I went out for a walk about midnight, but the snow wasn't sticking then. Why are you bothering with these details anyway, since the boy wasn't killed out here?"

Searcy raised his eyebrows. "Why do you say that?"

"No blood. Or very little. He had been lying out there for several hours, because the footprints of the killer had been covered up entirely, if there were any to begin with, so he must have been dumped not long after it began to snow. If he were still bleeding then, there would have been more blood. I imagine he got killed in the car, blunt instrument—as they say—and then the murderer drove around until he found just the right set of hemlocks to push him under."

"It's sort of dangerous though, isn't it, driving around with a dead man in the car?"

Lawrence shrugged. "Evidently not as dangerous as being a hustler. And, whoever it was did a smart thing in dumping the kid on private property rather than in a park somewhere, or dropping him off the bridge into the Mystic River."

"Why do you say that?"

"Because it confuses the issue. You drop a body onto somebody's lawn, and there's confusion, especially if the lawn belongs to somebody who has Connections with a capital C. That's what makes me think that whoever it was knew exactly where he was going. He may not have known Scarpetti personally, but he knew where he lived. On the other hand of course, you probably wouldn't be so down on all of this if Scarpetti weren't so important, so it may have been the stupidest thing to do, too. It could work either way."

"You've really thought this thing out," said Searcy with reluctant admiration.

"Murder is a hobby—at least since I moved in across from Mr. Scarpetti. It's just too bad that things had to work out quite the way they did—"

"How do you mean?"

"Well, it would have been better for everyone, I think, if instead of a faggot being found dead on Mr. Scarpetti's lawn—" Professor Lawrence paused pregnantly.

"Yes?"

"Mr. Scarpetti had been found bludgeoned to death on the Block. Scarpetti's not going to rest his head on his greasy pillow until he proves that this thing was a plot of the entire Boston homosexual community against him. He actually had the effrontery, when I first moved in here, to warn me to keep away from his fat pimply-faced cretinous twelve-year-old boy, as if I wouldn't shoot the child on sight, to the lasting benefit of humanity."

Searcy hesitated, consternated. "We've talked to the neighbors," he resumed after a moment, "but none of the others live as close as you. They didn't hear anything, didn't see anything, don't have any ideas. I was just wondering if you had."

Searcy stood and placed his cup on the edge of the table. Lawrence stood also, and followed Searcy into the hallway.

As Searcy was putting on his coat, Lawrence said, "There's one thing you can tell me about all this."

"What?"

"Newspaper this morning said the boy wasn't robbed—he had money in his back pocket."

"That's right. Thirty dollars, a ten and a twenty."

"Anything smaller?"

Searcy shook his head. "No ones, no change. Of course it could have been a robber, and the thief took everything out of the front pockets but forgot to check the back."

"That's not what I was getting at," said Lawrence. "Of course if a thief is going to be thorough enough to murder his victim, he's going to check *all* the pockets. You also found a white handkerchief with a lipstick smear on it."

"Yes," said Searcy, "what about it?"

"Well, just that the boy obviously came in contact with a woman sometime that night."

"How can you be sure? You ought to know that men have been known to use lipstick, especially—"

"The kid was wearing a jock-jacket, he wouldn't have been caught dead with lipstick—except of course that's exactly what happened. Besides, young hustlers only wear colored hand-kerchiefs. Do your homework. Somebody gave the kid that handkerchief."

"It could have belonged to somebody who was—in drag."

"Did you see the handkerchief?" demanded Lawrence.

"Yes, it was a plain white handkerchief with a lipstick smear in the center of it."

"Then it didn't belong to a drag. A drag would carry a woman's handkerchief, something frilly to wave about and show off. Otherwise she'd use Kleenex. Lieutenant, these days, only a straight woman would leave a lipstick smear on a plain white handkerchief."

"The kid was gay—" protested Searcy.

"The single point I've found in his favor," snapped Professor Lawrence, "at least insofar as he's been described in the papers—bad childhood, bad complexion, bad credit rating." Then, in a fine imitation of a little child's voice, he plaintively sang: "*Oh father's a drunkard and mother is dead...*" Then, abruptly resuming his normal low-pitched sonorous voice, he added: "Of course, now he has a second point in his favor."

"What's that?" said Searcy.

"He's caused Mario Scarpetti a great deal of trouble. I hear that the honorable representative's been getting calls of congratulations from people who think that *he* did it!"

Lawrence laughed, turned on the porch light, and opened the front door for Searcy.

Thursday, 4 January

Chapter Eight

"**F**IFTY-EIGHT." *Clap!* "Fifty-nine!" *Clap!* "Sixty!" *Clap!* Valentine paused before starting his fourth set of twenty push-ups. His arms were stretched out before him, pressed against the plushly carpeted exercise floor. In the long mirrored wall, he checked to be sure that his body was perfectly parallel to the floor. Not liking the way his toes bent in his red-striped Adidases, he straightened them, and thought, *Better...*At the International Health Spa, people noticed.

Five deep breaths were drawn into his lungs, and then released explosively. Valentine's hair lay flat against his head in damp waves. His red T-shirt and silver gym shorts were soaked through with perspiration. He held the sixth breath, and began another set of twenty push-ups, cursing himself for his first cigarette ten years before. Down, up, clap hands before he again smashed against the floor. To atone for his physical lassitude over the holidays, he didn't pause between the fourth and fifth sets, and counted steadily up to one hundred.

He dropped to the floor and rolled over onto his back, wondering if he would live. When he decided that he would, he did fifty sit-ups, and considered the question again. *No pain, no gain,* he told himself with a sneer.

He lay still until his pulse dropped below one hundred. He sat up, and inched backward till his spine pressed against the cool cement blocks of the long wall. He consciously relaxed all of his muscles, beginning at his toes and working upward.

He was well into his second hour of exercising and reflected that it was just as boring as he had anticipated. Thursday was not his usual day for a workout, but Wednesday's slow and difficult exercising had warned him that he had slipped over the holidays. An extra day was called for.

The gym was crawling with men: pushing-up, sitting-up, jumping rope, climbing rope, grappling with the horse and the parallel bars, or torturing their bodies on one of the Universal gym machines. Locked into the contraptions of steel bars and chrome springs, they looked to be victims of a trendy Inquisition as they attempted to expand thickly corded arms that didn't fit into the sleeves of their T-shirts as it was, and develop legs that would split the seams of their tight trousers as they rode their bicycles along the Esplanade.

Though set a little to one side, the bench press was the "center ring" of the place. For the straight men who visited the International Health Spa it was the essential element in foundation building, and they employed it to develop bulky, rounded upper bodies which, according to heterosexual lore, was the universal and infallible turn-on to beautiful women. Gay men, on the other hand, flocked to the defining equipment, the barbells and the U.G.M.s, after a short while on the bench press, to carve out their muscles, until, ideally, they resembled a page out of *Gray's Anatomy.*

In the International Health Spa the way to tell gay men from straight—and they were there in about equal numbers— was by the shape of their bodies. Gay men were trim and well-defined, but straight men had bulky chests, shoulders and upper arms, but suffered along with potting bellies, flabby buttocks, and spindly legs.

The wall behind Valentine vibrated slightly. Only a dozen feet above him was a suspended running track attached to the walls and the ceiling. He craned his head, trying to loosen the muscles there, and counted eleven men jogging around in unbroken rhythm.

Three of the men Valentine knew, but he liked only one: Randy Harmon. Valentine had not seen Randy since before the holidays, and had hoped to find him at the gym today. Disliking exercising with the same violent intensity, they often kept one another company there. "Misery loves visitors," Randy would say glumly as they changed into their gym clothes.

Valentine stood and moved to the middle of the floor, or as near as he could get without standing on a notorious muscle-exhibitionist who invariably took the center spot, and entertained and amazed all the novices with a display of the most complicated exercises for the lower stomach yet devised. He watched Randy's graceful athletic body go through the mechanical paces of running; he tried to catch his eye, but couldn't.

Randy Harmon was a couple of inches taller than Valentine; his hair, also reddish-blond, was worn short and he had a thick moustache some years old. When they had been roommates at Tufts, they were more than once mistaken for brothers, and though that no longer happened, they still bore a general physical similarity. Valentine waved a couple of times, but gave that over when he captured the attention of every man in the gym but Randy.

Valentine crossed the floor and climbed the metal stairs to the track. He leaned against the concrete wall, out of the way of the runners, who approached him from the left around the windowed corner. After the fourth passed, he stepped in without missing a beat. He did not see Randy at first, but then located him a few dozen yards ahead, just around the next bend. Rather than increasing his pace to catch up, Valentine decided it would be easier to drop his pace until Randy came up from behind. This took several minutes. He glanced over his shoulder when Randy was only a few yards back, but when Randy still showed no signs of recognizing him, Valentine fell into place beside his friend.

"I was looking for you earlier," gasped Valentine between breaths.

Randy continued to look straight ahead.

"Randy?" Valentine shouted and waved his hand in front of Randy's face.

Randy blinked and turned his head sharply; his face was expressionless. He stared at Valentine for a few seconds, then laughed, and broke his rhythm. He pointed to a little depression in the wall ahead, and he and Valentine fell away from the scattered group of runners and took shelter there.

Randy bent forward and pressed his splayed fingers against his muscular thighs and massaged them in long strokes to his knees. After a moment he straightened and took seven deep breaths, arching his back and spreading his arms to his side as he did so.

He turned to Valentine and smiled. "I hate all this."

Valentine nodded sympathetically. "I know. But you'll have to teach me your technique."

"Technique?"

"How to sleep with your eyes open and run at the same time."

"I just pretend I'm—" Randy turned his back on Valentine in the narrow space, lowered himself to the floor, and stretched his legs along the wall.

Valentine waited for him to finish the sentence. He didn't.

"Randy," said Valentine, "something wrong? Is your hypnotist playing tricks on you?"

"No," said Randy slowly, "I trust my hypnotist. It's something else. I—" He didn't finish that sentence either.

Behind Randy, Valentine dropped to his knees and peered over his friend's shoulder. "Randy, it's me—Val. If you don't tell me what's bothering you, I'm going to hamstring you."

Randy turned and drew his knees up under his chin. He cleared his throat. "OK—but you've got to be Tomb-mouth on this one—"

"Scratch my heart and hope to croak."

"Well," said Randy, "Sunday was New Year's Eve, and on Monday night this little hustler got his debts called in, and—"

Valentine closed his eyes and fell back against the wall. His feet slid underneath Randy's thighs. "Are you going to tell me a story about the Pig-man?"

Randy's brow creased. "What? Listen Valentine, if you don't—"

"You're going to tell me you got visited by Our Lady of the Pigpen? Searcy of the Waving Wand?"

"I didn't see his wand," said Randy. "How did you know?"

"And he pulled out a four-hundred-watt light bulb and ten feet of rubber hose, threatening you with the third degree—right?"

"You've run into him before then?"

"Yes."

"He showed up at the baths last night," said Randy.

Valentine laughed. "Searcy at the Royal Baths? I'll bet somebody was surprised to find that the bulge underneath his towel was a Magnum."

"It wasn't a social call, Val. Do me a favor, and shut up—I'm upset about this."

Valentine grimaced sympathetically. "He came in about William A. Golacinsky."

Randy nodded. "Worst possible time. Wednesday night is dollar night and every queen in town with four quarters to her name shows up. So, they're all lined up, all the way back to the elevator, and I'm checking 'em in, and this stud breaks in line, and everybody's saying, 'Well who does she think she is?' and then he waves a badge and ID in front of the window, and says, 'This is the police.' Well, that lobby emptied out like they were showing *Dark Victory* across the street. So I got Jerry to take over the window and took the cop in my office to talk."

"Did you know anything about Golacinsky?"

Randy hesitated and retied a lace that didn't need retying. "Yes, in fact I did. He was a regular, usually on the weekends. His weekends started on Wednesday."

Valentine sat up. "You *knew* him then?"

"I knew him like I know the other regulars. I didn't take him home to meet my parrot, if that's what you mean. He'd come in with a trick and the john would pay for the room. John would leave half an hour later, and Billy would leave the next morning."

"And he was there that Monday night?"

Randy nodded.

"Same formula? In with the john, john comes out, Billy leaves in the morning? And after that, I presume he takes the MTA out to the sticks, lays himself down under the hemlocks, bludgeons himself to death, and then hides the blunt instrument where fifty cops and an hysterical legislator can't lay their hands on it?"

"First part's right," said Randy. "In with john, but this time he leaves with john."

"Then you saw the guy he was with!"

"No—"

"Wait, I thought you—"

"Valentine," said Randy, with his arms outstretched before him, "you mind if we continue this in the sauna? The vibrations here are giving me a headache."

They ran one lap more around the trembling platform, and then descended the metal stairs.

Valentine and Randy showered quickly, threw their towels over their shoulders and entered the sauna. They took seats on the top tier, carefully searching out a section of bench without splinters, but didn't say anything until the two men already there had left.

Valentine checked his pulse. It was up again. He dropped down a tier, where the temperature was not much more than 150°.

"I hate hassles," said Randy, "and that cop hassled me."

Valentine said nothing for a moment, then asked, "Was he drinking?"

Randy shrugged. "Maybe. I don't know. I can't smell anything. He could have been gargling Aqua Velva and I wouldn't have known it. He wasn't slamming off the wall, if that's what you mean, and he could apparently walk a straight line. But he was—belligerent."

"What did he say when you said you couldn't remember what john looked like?"

"He didn't believe me. You know, you're behind the counter and you're thinking about going home in half an hour, so you take their money, look at the membership card, make out the time check, and buzz 'em on inside. You don't even look at 'em. At two in the morning, who cares?"

"Then how'd you know it was Billy, if you didn't look up?"

Randy laughed. "You know what his card says? It says 'Duke Wayne' on it. I didn't think anybody bothered using a fake name these days, especially not a bus station hustler. I remember when he bought the card, he hesitated before writing his name on the back. Duke Wayne? No punky little kid with bad skin is called Duke Wayne, for Christ's sake. I wouldn't call my dog Duke Wayne, and she's dead. So when I saw the card come across the counter it was Billy. I heard somebody call him that one time, and that's how I know Billy was his name. Anyway, I could see john out of the corner of my eye. He was standing to one side, with his back to me, as if he didn't want me to see his face."

"How long did Billy stay?"

"They got a room, but in twenty minutes Billy was back at the desk, dressed, and he threw the keys on the counter and went to the elevator, mad. Even forgot to take his card back. I was looking this time, because I knew that something had gone wrong. John joined him—no, I *can't* remember john's name. They didn't say a word, looked like a lover's quarrel."

"But did you see the john then?"

Randy sighed and sat forward. He swept the perspiration from his thighs and flung it onto the hot rocks in the deep tray beside the door. It evaporated with a loud sizzle.

"Medium height, gray hair, overcoat..."

"And?"

"That's it. He kept his back to me. They got on the elevator and left. Maybe I would have been more curious if I hadn't been so busy. So that's what I told Searcy. And I gave him the membership card that said 'Duke Wayne' on it."

"And Searcy said—"

"Searcy said I was lying. He said I was the last person to see Billy alive, and that I was protecting the murderer. Covering up the trail. He said if I wasn't down at Berkeley Street with a full description and telephone number of that guy he'd have me charged with conspiracy and withholding of evidence."

"He can't do that."

"Of course not. But you remember my old boyfriend Cal? He's a lawyer—his firm represents Clarisse's office. Anyway, I called him up, and if Searcy comes back with any more threats, I'm just supposed to give him Cal's card." He shrugged dismally. "I'm not afraid of Searcy for that, because I can take care of myself, and the time is past somebody like him can come in and push me around just because I'm gay. No judge in town would listen to him for more than five minutes. But like I say, it's the hassle. I don't like having to carry around Cal's card in my wallet all the time, and I certainly don't like the man coming around flashing his badge."

Valentine sighed heavily. "I wouldn't worry about it now. Searcy's just blowing off steam because he hasn't got any leads. He's got problems of his own. Mario Scarpetti is probably onto the cops every waking minute. Now, I talked to Searcy a couple of times, and he's got a problem. He got put on this investigation in the gay community, and he thought he was going to come down on top of all these squishy little faggots and strike terror in our hearts, and from what it sounds like, nobody's getting struck with terror. He's getting pushed himself, and so he's pushing you."

"Yeah, he did that too."

"He laid hands on you?"

"He shoved me up against the wall."

"What did you do?"

"I said, 'When do you get off duty?' He said, 'I'm off duty now.' So then I shoved him back, hard. I knew better than to raise my hand to a cop that's on duty, even if there weren't any witnesses. He's in decent shape—more than decent shape—but he's not as quick as I am. He stormed out and said he'd better see me on Berkeley Street by Friday or my ass was cooked. Cal said it was just possible he could drag me into court, if he's really crazy, but I don't want it to go that far. I hate hassles."

Valentine raised himself onto the top tier again. The two men then arranged themselves lengthwise on the narrow bench, leaning against either end of the small timbered room, facing one another. The heat was exhausting.

Randy knitted his brows. "The problem is..."

"What?" urged Valentine.

"The problem is, that after that cop left I thought of something else, but I'm afraid to call him up again because he'll think I was holding back on purpose, and that I know even more."

"What was it you remembered?"

"Billy's john. He had a bag of toys."

Valentine said nothing.

"Actually, I don't know what he had inside. Like a doctor's bag, maybe not as big, black leather. And I remember thinking: he had something in there that Billy didn't want to play with, and that's why they argued. But Valentine, what if he didn't have just toys inside that bag? What if he wasn't carrying around 'marital aids'? What if he had a hammer or a lead pipe?"

Chapter Nine

CLARISSE LOVELACE waited patiently for Daniel Valentine in the lobby of the International Health Spa. She was a member herself, but men and women had separate exercise rooms, and she wasn't as faithful in her attendance as Valentine. She examined now—as she had often examined before—one of the large paintings that flanked the wide entrance. This pair of large canvases, of the German academic school of the mid-nineteenth century, depicted the youth of Imperial Rome enjoying decorous physical activity in shimmering togas. In Clarisse's favorite, two blond men and a lithe young woman played an elaborate game of hoops. The scene lay in a large grove of unidentifiable trees, with the portico of a magnificent villa and the Mediterranean visible here and there through the foliage. Dappled sunlight illuminated the golden heads of the three participants. The two men appeared to be twins—because the painter couldn't afford more than one model, Clarisse assumed—and she was attracted to both. Studying their features and expressions in detail, she realized that she liked them simply because they resembled a beardless Valentine.

She sighed. Valentine was at once as close and as unattainable as the two men of oil and canvas.

Clarisse had never come so near Daniel Valentine as during their brief intimacy in Bermuda, when his sexual orientation had not been so settled a question as now. But when she discovered that his impotency in her bed was counterbalanced with extreme prowess with the assistant manager of the hotel, Clarisse collapsed with grief, rage, and embarrassment, and took the first flight home. But back in Boston, Valentine had called her up and, oddly, from the moment she first heard his voice on the phone, the rift had been closed. They were fast companions since that time, and their friendship was broken only every couple of years or so by some violent pointless argument.

She pulled her fur coat close about her shoulders and turned away from the painting. Valentine approached silently across the double-laid Oriental carpets. He was hurriedly pulling on his navy pea coat over a red hooded sweatshirt.

"I'm late," he apologized.

She shrugged noncommittally, and buttoned her coat as they moved toward the wide glass doors. They didn't speak as they descended the dark, short flight of stairs. They had just stepped out in the frigid night air when Valentine hurried to the edge of the street, stooped, and lifted a torn playing card from a pile of snow and ice atop a storm drain. He thumped it with his forefinger to loosen the filth on it, and slipped it into the pocket of his pea jacket.

"God!" breathed Clarisse, "how can I maintain my facade as a woman of fashion and leisure if I keep company with a man who picks playing cards up out of the gutter?"

"Ten of spades. Congress. Blue field, red filigree border. Probably part of a bridge set."

They dodged traffic to cross to the boulevard down the center of Commonwealth Avenue. Invariably they preferred this generous path to the much narrower sidewalk in front of the townhouses on either side of the street. Bare gnarled oaks and maples lined the island, and new street-lamps burned sharply behind their black branches. Daniel still said nothing, but as they were crossing Fairfield Street, Clarisse slipped her arm into his.

"What's the matter? You gain five pounds over the holidays?"

He laughed shortly. "No, in fact I lost."

"What's wrong then?"

He took a package of cigarettes from his pocket. They paused beneath the statue of a bald man who had once done something, or said something, or caused something to happen quite by accident. Valentine lit one for himself and offered a second to Clarisse. She took it.

"I saw Randy Harmon at the gym," he said.

"Randy's always at the gym. It's hard to believe him anymore when he tries to tell you how much he hates it."

Valentine, as they moved on, more slowly now, told Clarisse about Lieutenant Searcy's raucous visit to the Royal Baths.

"Well," said Clarisse, "at least he's living up to his name."

"Still think he's cute?"

"I see the man's point. How could Randy not have noticed the john? I mean, he was interested enough to notice how long Billy stayed with him, and notice that he was carrying a bag of toys."

Valentine shrugged. "Think, though, Clarisse. He just didn't. Just the way that I tune out the people who come to Bonaparte's. It's automatic. There's such a thing as too much information—too much input. You don't *want* to know all your customers. They order a drink, you fix it, you take the money, and it's on to the next. The regulars I remember, but even that takes time."

"You sound like a whore," said Clarisse.

Where Commonwealth Avenue ends, at Arlington Street, they stopped for crossing traffic. Clarisse pressed Valentine's arm. "OK, I know you're upset and I feel bad for Randy, but Randy's just going to have to take care of himself, and we should all be so lucky as to have an ex who's as good a lawyer as Cal.

But tonight we're going to have a nice dinner together, just you and I, and put all this aside. Tomorrow you have off. You have dinner with me, and then I'll spin you around three times and send you out to a bar and you can pick up the most beautiful man in Boston."

Valentine smiled warmly. "If you weren't a woman, I'd marry you. Where do we eat?"

"I don't care. Let's try the Tudor House. We haven't been there for at least two weeks."

"All right. Bonaparte's first though. The Tudor House doesn't have a license."

There was a small boisterous crowd at Bonaparte's when Valentine and Clarisse arrived. Someone was going away somewhere, or had just returned, or had been fired from a job he didn't like—at any rate, someone and all his friends were very drunk.

Valentine and Clarisse did not check their coats but settled immediately into two seats in the main bar downstairs, as far as possible from those celebrating. Jack brought Clarisse her usual scotch and water and Valentine ordered a beer.

After the scotch touched her lips, Clarisse's eyes blew open in panic. She gripped Valentine's arm, spilling his beer. "Oh, my God!" she cried.

"What is it?"

"I forgot to call in sick today."

"It's a little late, don't you think?"

Clarisse wiped up the beer with a bar napkin and threw it at Jack. "No," she said with determination, "it's never too late."

She slid off the stool and crossed through the Wicker Room. She leaned against the wall between the two restroom doors and dropped a dime into the pay telephone there. While waiting for the real estate office's answering service to respond, she noted that although Trudy was not at the keyboard, several sheets of music were strewn across the top of the piano. There was a line of three empty glasses on the edge of the bench. She remembered then that Trudy's weekly sing-along began at eight each Thursday night; it was the only thing for which Trudy was on time.

Clarisse shifted her envelope from one arm to the other. After fifteen rings a female with an offensive Boston accent answered huffily. Clarisse identified herself and then dictated a message. "I am writhing in bed with the flu, doped up on Contac, and waiting for a team of surgeons." At the end, she said, "Sign that—'Lovelace, eight-thirty A.M.'"

The woman protested the inaccuracy of the time, but Clarisse was stern. She got her way.

Pleased, Clarisse replaced the receiver and turned. The contact lens in her left eye slipped from her iris, and without hesitation she whirled about and stiff-armed her way into the ladies room.

Clarisse plugged the sink and drew a couple of inches of lukewarm water. She leaned toward the mirror, and tried to right the lens with a wetted finger.

The lens was replaced. To check it, she focused first on her own image in the mirror, then on the two stalls behind her. In the one adjacent to the outside wall, there was a sudden commotion of rustling material and a violent repeated sigh of exasperation.

Clarisse turned, curious, and leaned against the sink. Through the crack by the door, she could see flashing stuffs of light green, dark green, and black.

"Oh, Jesus!" cried a deep masculine voice from the stall.

The sound of snapped elastic crackled through the small room, and was immediately followed by an even greater commotion of rustling material. Clarisse wondered for a moment whether there were a Girl Scout troop in crinolines behind the door.

There was a splash.

"Oh, God!" cried the voice.

Clarisse folded her arms and leaned back against the sink.

The door to the stall was eased open, and Trudy's light-blue wig, the color of Cinderella's ball-dress in the Disney film, emerged askew. Beneath it, Trudy's green-lashed eyes fluttered up. "Oh, Clarisse, I'm glad it's just you. I thought one of my fans had come in to attack."

Trudy grabbed Clarisse's arm, and pulled herself entirely out of the stall. Clarisse pushed her over to the other sink. "Is life hard, Trudy?" asked Clarisse sympathetically.

Trudy leaned against the sink and sighed. The green plastic lashes above and below her eyes meshed like gears. "Life is a shambles," she whispered.

"Worse than usual?"

"The strap on my new brassiere broke, right in the middle of 'Lucy in the Sky with Diamonds.' I was so humiliated I couldn't even finish, and it was a request. Half of me was up here where it should be, and the other one was down there around my girdle. Then, when I was in there"—she pointed one broken green nail at the stall—"I was putting Mama's Helper back in, and the damn thing fell in the toilet! Oh, Clarisse," Trudy moaned, "I think I'm being punished for all my unpaid parking tickets. I haven't had to stuff my brassiere with toilet tissue since my high school graduation!"

Clarisse wanted desperately to ask whether Trudy had graduated from high school in drag, but she forbore in consideration of Trudy's distress.

Trudy straightened herself, put on a brave face, and turned to the mirror. She smoothed the material of her dress over her hips. She studied her breasts critically, and adjusted the left slightly, moving it to the side. Then she moved the other in the same direction. "Honey," she said, "if I thought this bra would fit you, I'd take it off right now and strap it on you. Aren't you uncomfortable bouncing around like that? Don't take this the wrong way, but they're not—*discreet*, if you know what I mean."

Clarisse rolled her eyes and pursed her mouth. She drew her coat closed. "I rent more flats if I don't wear a bra," she said tightly.

Trudy shrugged. "As long as you don't mind a little curvature of the spine, I guess it's all right. How do I look?"

Trudy turned slightly to one side, and then to the other; Clarisse looked her up and down appraisingly. "Fine," she said, "you're just where you should be. But where's your lipstick?"

Trudy looked away, and touched her mouth nervously. "I gave it up—New Year's resolution. A little fat girl at the cosmetic counter at Filene's told me lipstick was out this season." Trudy pulled absently at the curls at the back of her wig.

Clarisse opened her envelope and pulled out a comb; she ran it slowly and thoughtfully through her thick black hair. Out of the corner of her eye, through the mirror's image, she watched Trudy examining her lashes and straightening the wide collar of her green blouse.

Clarisse put the comb away, and pulled out a tube of lipstick. She uncapped it and turned the tube up; carefully she applied it to her lips. She felt Trudy's eyes on her.

"Nice color," said Trudy.

Clarisse smacked, and smiled broadly to test her outlines. "'Savage Cerise.' Only at Bonwit's."

"I wonder if they would have the shade that I used to wear all the time," said Trudy. "It was darker than yours, and brighter, and it had maybe just a little purple in it. It was so hard finding something that went with green."

"What is it called?"

Trudy shrugged. "I don't know. Vermilion something."

Clarisse turned and looked at Trudy. "You've worn it for five years, at least. How can you not know what it's called?"

"Well," replied Trudy, "my wife used to buy it for me, half-dozen tubes at a time, and mail order. Nobody could beat Rochelle when it came to color-coordination. I wouldn't think of leaving the house until she had looked me over. Well, when Rochelle knew she was about to—pass over—she ordered two dozen for me. She asked if I wanted her to order more, but I said no, that by the time that I had used them up, I'd be dead of grief. I've run out now, or almost—I'm saving the last tube for whoever does my face for the coffin. I'd order more myself, but the dog went wild after Rochelle—kicked off—and ate all the order blanks." Trudy smiled sadly.

"You must miss Rochelle."

"Next year would have been our fortieth anniversary— that's rubies. We were planning on identical outfits. Rochelle was the best seamstress I ever met. We wore the same size, a perennial ten, both of us. And there couldn't be anything more convenient than that. Life is a drag without Rochelle..." She took a deep breath and straightened herself. "Well," she said bravely, "it's not New Year's anymore. Let me borrow your lipstick, doll."

Clarisse handed her the tube, and Trudy applied it with abandon. "Death," she said, staring at her mouth in the mirror, "is a bad trip to lay on somebody you love."

"Yes," said Clarisse vaguely, rummaging in her envelope, "like that poor little hustler in the bushes."

"Yes," said Trudy, after a two-beat pause, "he had everything against him. Bad skin, thin shoes—"

"And somebody who wanted him dead."

"Nobody wanted him dead. He had just turned nineteen. Just a little boy..."

"In his trade," said Clarisse, "nineteen was hardly a spring chicken. More like a roaster. Did you know him?"

Trudy looked at Clarisse briefly in the mirror. She recapped the lipstick, and handed it back. "Of course not. What kind of people do you think I hang out with? A working grandmother doesn't have time to hang around with little boys who sell their bodies for profit."

Clarisse shrugged. "You talked about him as if you knew him, as if you were sorry he was dead."

Discomfort crossed Trudy's face. She grabbed at the waist of her skirt and pulled it up. "Of course I'm sorry he's dead. The dead die young, and all that. God, my panty hose are driving me crazy!" She turned violently and wiggled her hips. "Don't ever think you're saving money by buying cheap panty hose. The elastic always breaks at just the wrong time. Did I ever tell you about my Waterloo with panty hose?"

"Ah...no you didn't, Trudy."

"Well," she sighed. She released her skirt, smoothed it neatly over her curving hips. She pushed Clarisse out the door and followed her into the Wicker Room. "It was in Provincetown, about three years ago—"

Trudy crossed and sat at the piano. The three empty glasses had been removed and another drink had been placed on a cocktail napkin beside her music stand. She sipped at it. "—and I went to see Martin Drake, who does the best Joan Crawford act you ever saw in your life. We were old friends, and he had gotten me a ringside seat. I was wearing my tuxedo dress outfit—very chic that summer. So Martin finished re-creating the first dressing room scene in *All About Eve*—his Thelma Ritter is flawless—and he makes 'em put the spotlight on me, and introduces me as having the best set of legs in Provincetown..." Trudy turned on the piano bench, and crossed her legs at the knee, displaying them to Clarisse. "Well, all the boys—and half of 'em I didn't even know—started chanting 'Trudy, Trudy, Trudy' and Martin begged me to come up with him. So two waiters lifted me up on the stage, and the boys all cried out, 'Show us your gams, Trudy! Show us your gams!' So I played the band to beat Miss Grable, and hiked up my skirt—" She swallowed half her drink.

"And?" coaxed Clarisse.

"—Not a whisper in the house. They were stunned, and I thought, 'My legs aren't *that* good.' Then they started to laugh. I raised my skirt higher. Martin picked up the mike and said 'Put your skirt down, Trudy, your twosies are hanging out.' God, they still talk about it on Commercial Street. I won't go down there anymore. Last June I was there and some little boy leaned out of a car and shouted, 'Show us your twosies, Trudy!' Always buy the best," concluded Trudy sententiously.

"Well," said. Clarisse, "it must have been embarrassing, but it's not the kind of thing that's likely to happen to me."

"I suppose not," said Trudy, and turned with a small smile to the piano.

Clarisse realized how long she had neglected Valentine, and turned back to the bar. She saw him leaning forward, in close conversation with Jack; but a couple of feet behind his back was an enormous package, done up in bright red foil paper and wide gold ribbon tied in a grotesquely large bow. It was held by a well-built man with black hair and a full black moustache. The man wore a heavy black leather jacket, new-pressed jeans, and heavy mud-stained work boots. The hands holding the package were strong and wide, with thick dark hair across the backs. All his strong fine features were smiling.

"What's *that*?" whispered Trudy.

"Oh, God!" mumbled Clarisse, and moved away from Trudy without answering.

Jack had stopped listening to Valentine and was staring over his shoulder. Valentine turned about on the stool.

"Happy birthday!" cried the man holding the package.

"Mark!" exclaimed Valentine.

Clarisse stood between the men smiling pleasantly. "Hello, Mark," she said, "we're *so* glad you made it."

He nodded, still smiling, but didn't take his eyes from Valentine.

In the Wicker Room, Trudy struck up a florid version of "Happy Birthday," and the entire bar joined in on the second line. The song was repeated with increased fervor; Trudy ended with a flourish and everyone applauded.

Valentine was flushed. "I'm a Libra," he whispered. "I was born in October." No one paid attention.

Mark stepped forward and placed the package across Valentine's lap. He bent forward, took Valentine's aggrieved face gently in his hands and kissed him hard on the mouth. Valentine tried to pull back, but wasn't allowed to. There was applause throughout the thirty-second embrace.

"Break it up," cried Clarisse. "You're steaming the mirrors."

"Mark," gasped Valentine, "it was very thoughtful of you, but, you know, it's not my birthday."

Mark unzipped his jacket, and threw himself onto the stool beside Valentine. "I know, but I wanted an excuse to give you something."

"Open it, Val," demanded Clarisse. She stood beside Mark, with her hand gently on his shoulder. Valentine untied the ribbon and pulled the red foil aside. Clarisse took the discarded paper, wadded it, and threw it at Jack.

Valentine pulled open the top of the box, and lifted out a waist-length jacket. It was of shining dark-brown leather, had zippered pockets, a wide collar, and dark-fur lining.

"It's gorgeous, Mark, but you shouldn't have put your money into something like this for me."

"Don't be rude," said Clarisse.

Valentine laid the jacket across his lap and rested his hand on Mark's thigh. "I don't deserve this, I—"

"You deserve it, for just being who you are—"

Behind Mark's back, Clarisse rolled her eyes. She snatched the coat out of Valentine's lap to display it to the curious and admiring onlookers.

"—and besides, I have a friend who does them. He practically gave it to me, when I told him who it was for. I mean, when I told him how much you meant to me, and how much I wanted to give you something."

"Well, I appreciate it, Mark. In fact, I love the jacket."

Clarisse had turned back. "Yes," she said, "maybe now you can pass for butch."

Valentine ignored her remark. He removed his pea coat and reached out for the jacket. A man who had been rubbing the fur lining against his cheek and exclaiming its softness handed the gift back to Valentine. He slipped it on, said it fit perfectly, and turned to examine his appearance in the mirror behind the bar.

Trudy played "Easter Parade" until Valentine gave her the finger, and then she modulated into "I Enjoy Being a Girl," which was greeted with even greater laughter. Valentine ignored it.

"I love the coat," said Valentine to Mark.

Mark nodded happily. "I'm glad," he whispered.

"We have to talk," said Valentine. "Not right now, not here, but later."

"Oh, sure," said Mark.

"Clarisse and I are going out to eat. Come with us."

Mark held up his hands. "I stopped on the way. Lumberjacks eat early. I'm dead too, been up since four. Can I drop my pack at your place and lie down for a while? I could use a shower too."

Valentine detached his keys from his back belt loop and handed them to Mark. "Take your time. Why don't we meet at the Eagle about midnight. I guess we can talk there as well as anywhere else."

Mark nodded and stood. He squeezed Valentine's arm affectionately, smiled at Clarisse, and was gone.

Clarisse fingered the collar of the coat. "Most beautiful wedding ring I've ever seen."

Valentine whipped about on the stool. "Rye," he said to Jack, "straight up. And pour a bottle of Perrier over Loveless's head."

"That's Love*lace*, creep."

Jack brought drinks for them both and after remaining silent for several moments, Clarisse turned to Valentine and blurted, "Oh, guess what!"

"What?"

"I caught some of the noontime news on the TV, and guess who was on it?"

"The five top winners in the Mamie Van Doren look-alike contest."

"No," said Clarisse, "just the second runner-up: Mario Scarpetti."

"Oh, God!" cried Valentine, "what did he say?"

"Well, of course they asked him about the dead boy in the bush, and he went into this tirade about the 'homosexual element' in Boston, and how it had lowered the moral climate and property values and raised the tax rate, and if we didn't stop it, this place was going to be worse than California, and we weren't going to have any blue laws, and we'd be seeing unwashed men kissing each other on park benches, and everyone would have to send his children to Catholic schools because that's the only place where homosexuals couldn't get at 'em—"

"Oh ho," interrupted Valentine miserably, "I should introduce him to that hot priest from Fall River that I carried home Saturday night. He was late for mass because I made him help me scrape the Crisco off the walls on Sunday morning."

"Anyway," said Clarisse, "during the commercial, they had to wipe the foam off his mouth..."

While she talked, a tall, dark-complexioned man with straight black hair and a small moustache had entered the bar and taken the stool next to Valentine's. He wore a denim jacket and a heavy black sweater beneath it. After ordering a beer from Jack, he and Clarisse exchanged brief, almost startled nods over Valentine's head.

Valentine slid his empty glass toward Jack. "Anybody been in here looking for me?"

"No. Are you expecting someone?"

"Maybe," said Valentine. "He's tall, fat, got pink skin and bristles, a little round snout and big pointy ears that you can't make a silk purse out of. He's got beady eyes and a badge."

The man next to Valentine laughed.

"What?" said Jack.

"A cop named Searcy. Watch out. He's been coming down hard this week."

"You expect him in here?" said Jack nervously.

"No. Maybe. You haven't seen me. He'd be wanting to talk about that little hustler that got killed."

The man in the denim jacket and the black sweater made a noisy movement. His brow furrowed, and he guzzled down half his beer. He nervously pocketed his change and dropped off the stool.

Clarisse, having watched all in the mirror behind the bar, turned and stared after the man who rushed past the checkroom and out into the cold January night.

Chapter Ten

THE TUDOR HOUSE was a restaurant, seating about seventy-five, on the ground and second floors of a converted townhouse on Newbury Street. It had walnut paneling, leaded-glass windows, and middle-aged waitresses. Its menu was known less for the items on it, which were of the standard beef-and-potatoes variety, than for its pricings which were arbitrary and peculiar. Creamed corn for instance was forty-seven cents, while the complete liver-and-bacon dinner was four dollars and one cent.

Valentine and Clarisse were seated at a small table cramped into the leaded-glass embrasure that looked out over the Newbury Street sidewalk. Their waitress was a tall slender woman with short platinum hair, a pale soft complexion, and wide light-blue eyes. She smiled as she edged her way toward them. Leaning forward and resting her palms on the edge of their table, so that it was in danger of overturning, she said, "Well, haven't see you two in a while. D'you have a nice Christmas?"

"We went to the Yucatan," said Clarisse. "It was great." She slid her coat off her shoulders, and it fell over the back of the chair.

"You look tired, Marie," said Valentine.

Marie smiled again, and showed off her perfect teeth. "My feet are screaming," she said.

Clarisse glanced at the menu briefly. "The chicken and black coffee. No appetizer. Salad with Russian. You choose the dessert."

"German chocolate," said Marie, and scribbled on her pad.

"Herring and coffee," said Valentine. "Tomato soup, no salad, German chocolate for me too."

"Sounds awful," said Marie, and scribbled again. "Cook's going to come out here and shoot you dead, ordering herring and tomato soup. I'll be back in a minute." Marie edged through the tables, skillfully ignoring a woman who desperately wanted her check.

Valentine rested back in his chair and peered out onto Newbury Street. The fashionable small shops and boutiques were all closed at this hour, but the street was fairly busy with couples wandering from one lighted window to another. Most passersby stopped at the display of the shop next to the Tudor House in which seven formally attired female mannequins were threatening one another with ice trays.

Valentine watched carefully the dismay of two young women who had stopped in front of the window. *Students,* thought Valentine. *Boston University, School of Applied Music, 700 Commonwealth Avenue, one has a boyfriend who's a trumpet player, the other is a closet lesbian.* They moved on before he could delve any deeper into their obvious lives.

Valentine turned back to Clarisse. She was smoking. She drew in on the cigarette and let the smoke waft from her mouth in soft curls. She stared at him with weary eyes.

Valentine didn't smile, but he said, "Ida Lupino."

Clarisse nodded, shaking her hair so that one dark wave fell down over her right eye. "Right. But what film?"

Valentine cocked his head, and closed one eye. "Ummmmm. *They Drive by Night.*"

"You're too good," she said, and pushed her hair back.

"Who was that man?"

"Which man?" said Clarisse, glancing out the window.

"At Bonaparte's. Black hair, denim jacket, black sweater."

"He's a neurosurgeon at Mass General. He was the last person to see Vivien Leigh alive."

Marie brought two cups of steaming coffee. Clarisse and Valentine nodded thanks, and Valentine said then, "No. Who was he?"

"You want the story?" She smiled and raised her eyebrows.

Valentine shrugged. "Sure."

"You're not interested in him, are you? *Interested*, I mean."

"No."

"His name's Frank Hougan. I've never told you about him?"

"No," said Valentine, with impatience. "So tell me. He rented his flat from you, right?"

"A year ago, maybe more. I was at work one day, and he came by with his girlfriend. His girlfriend's name is Boots, Boots Slater."

"Boots...?" said Valentine skeptically.

"Yes," said Clarisse, "and as it turned out, 'Whips-and-Chains' would have been just as accurate." Clarisse smiled then for the first time. Valentine leaned forward now with more interest. They both laughed.

"You've seen her," said Clarisse in a low conspiratorial voice. "A little shorter than I, skinny, long straight brown hair. Keeps her hair shoved up under a black leather motorcycle hat."

"Does she ride a motorcycle?"

"She's usually so stoned, it's all she can do to ride an escalator without losing her feet in the treads. Always wears black leather—hat, vest, pants, boots, has a heart outlined in golden studs on her crotch."

Valentine nodded ruefully. "I followed her three blocks once, thinking she was a hot new man in town. Then I saw the darts. I see her now and again, lurching along, but only at night."

"Bride of Dracula. Sunlight does nasty things to her skin."

"So what else do you know about them?" demanded Valentine.

"Well, they came in looking for an apartment, both of 'em dressed in black, both of 'em with dark glasses, even though it was late afternoon and the sky was overcast, and Hougan said he wanted something with lots of room and a beamed ceiling. Didn't care about anything else. Didn't care if there was a fireplace, or a view, or a kitchen big enough for more than two cockroaches at once—but he had to have a beamed ceiling. So I went through our files, and showed him everything we had with a beamed ceiling. Took him to Jamaica Plain, but that was too far out. Showed him a place on Louisberg Square, but that wasn't big enough. Finally found a place on Commonwealth Avenue with beams in every room. Even the bathroom had beams—he *loved* that. All that took two days."

"And?"

"So they signed the lease, or rather Hougan signed the lease, and they moved in. Rent was always on time. It's one of the buildings we manage—one of *my* buildings in fact. They never complained about light bulbs going out in the hallway or the radiator exploding or anything like that. But then the neighbors started calling."

Clarisse paused dramatically.

Valentine refused to coax her on.

They both sipped their coffee for a couple of moments, and sat back for the arrival of Valentine's soup and Clarisse's salad.

"Mr. Hougan and Ms. Slater were running an ad in the *Phoenix* classifieds. You read those things, so you're bound to have seen it. 'Leather master and leather mistress will make pleasure out of your pain. You'll crawl away satisfied. No scene too far out. Will work separately or together. Men or women or couples welcome. Well-equipped play room. Reasonable rates. Visa, Master Charge, other major credit cards accepted.' Well, the place became a parade ground of perversion, two or three people a night, all hours."

"And the little old ladies across the street complained about what they could see through their windows?"

"No. But the people in the building got tired of muffled groans of ecstasy and whiplashes in the night. People pleading, and people screaming, and people swinging from the chains they had attached to the beams."

Valentine laughed. "What'd you do?"

"Well, I called 'em up. I *had* to. Fortunately, I got hold of Boots, and I told her, straight out, that it didn't bother me if they wanted to beat people up for profit, but that they were making too much noise."

"Was she mad?"

"No," said Clarisse. "She was very sweet. She apologized, said she didn't know that the noise traveled like that, and that they would put up soundproofing. Evidently they did, because there hasn't been a complaint in the last six months. And the ad's still running."

"Yes," said Valentine, "it's in this week's paper. Why didn't you tell me about them before?"

"I think when all this happened, you and I weren't speaking. That's why I didn't tell you."

Valentine nodded, then said, "You were surprised to see him tonight."

"Yes," said Clarisse, "I assumed he was straight. I mean, he's probably kinky enough to do anything as long as it pays, but he didn't strike me as the kind to go to a gay bar, and certainly not Bonaparte's. He was probably just as surprised to see me there. I thought it was a little strange in fact that he remembered me at all."

"I saw him in the mirror," said Valentine. "Then I was talking to Jack about Searcy. Hougan started to say something, and then he changed his mind."

"He left in a hurry," said Clarisse.

"Because I mentioned Searcy."

"No," said Clarisse, "he left when you mentioned Billy the Dead Boy."

Valentine smiled as Marie removed his soup plate and replaced it with a plate of herring salad. "The cook hates your guts," she said, and went smiling away.

"Well," said Clarisse, spearing a shred of chicken with her fork, "you think you ought to say anything to Searcy?"

"Say what? That a man in a black sweater left the bar when I mentioned his name?"

Clarisse shrugged. "You're right. He was probably just late for an appointment."

"Yeah," said Valentine, "somebody was going to pay him five dollars to walk on his face with cleats."

Chapter Eleven

BOLSTERED AGAINST the cold by the Tudor House's German chocolate cake, Valentine and Clarisse strolled leisurely down Newbury Street, crossing from one side to the other several times in the length of each block to stare into the windows of their favorite shops. Valentine was particularly taken with a large penguin driving a racing car in the display of F.A.O. Schwarz, and Clarisse desperately wanted to possess a Chinese laundry basket fashioned in the likeness of Donald Duck. But, arm in arm, looking for all the world like an affianced couple in the "Living" section of the Sunday *Globe*, they paused longest before the window of a small dress shop, whose branches were located in Palm Beach and Milan. In it, a leggy mannequin attired in high '40s style stood on the unhinged door of a star's dressing room while an adoring fan (or perhaps her husband) lay crushed beneath it.

"It's an allegory of Time," Clarisse explained.

Valentine pulled her to the next shop, where they studied the high-contrast black-and-white photographs of the latest and most fashionable hairstyles. Clarisse pulled her thick black hair back, and pushed it up, while examining her reflection carefully in the smoked glass of the shop's window.

"You think I would look more like Faye Dunaway if I cut it all off?"

"No, but if you bleached it nobody'd be able to tell you from Diana Dors."

Clarisse opened her hand. The waves of her black hair fell softly about her furred shoulders. "I'd look awful with short hair. Like Glenda Jackson when she's not smiling."

"Or Marjorie Main when she is."

They moved farther up the street. "But the real question," said Clarisse, "is what are you going to do about Mark?"

"I'm going to break it to him gently. 'Mark, I like you, I don't love you. Give me a call sometime. Good-bye.' And then, so that he won't feel so bad, I'll see him off at the bus in the morning."

"Where's he going to sleep tonight?"

Valentine laughed. "I've never thrown anything that looked like *that* out of my bed!"

"That's encouraging him."

"He'll sleep on the couch." Valentine fingered the zipper of his new jacket. "You don't think I should offer to return the coat, do you?"

"He'd be hurt."

"Good," said Valentine, "then I won't even offer. He might take me up on it."

"Doesn't it make you feel the tiniest bit obligated, that he gave you a jacket tonight—in the presence of witnesses—that would cost you one-seventy-five on the open market?"

"Well," said Valentine, and then paused. "Maybe I won't make him sleep on the couch after all. The trouble is, he's not going to want to *sleep* at all."

Clarisse hurried him up Exeter Street. "One more look at the Christmas tree—they take it down tomorrow."

Boylston Street was busy with foot traffic, especially right around the jazz bars and the liquor stores. A fat bearded man was distributing questionnaires on the state of passersby's souls; two young women with long straight hair were playing a recorder duet near the entrance of Burger King; and drunks were taking shelter with their bottles of Thunderbird in the recessed doorways of banks and travel agencies. Tourists stumbled along dazedly, afraid to ask directions. A disco version of "We Three Kings of Orient Are" filled the sidewalk outside of Strawberries record store, but as they continued uptown it was gradually overtaken by more traditional versions of Christmas carols that poured out of windswept Prudential Plaza.

There, Valentine stood behind Clarisse with his ungloved hands deep in the pockets of her fur coat. They stared up at the tremendous blue spruce. The sixty-foot tree was covered over with tiny twinkling colored lights, and a star the size of a high-seas distress signal was perched at the top. Chubby white plastic winged cherubs with white lights in their bellies were scattered among the branches. The wind whipping around the base of the tall building stirred the branches and the cherubs seemed coyly to pursue one another through the greenery. "Jesus Bambino" in a reed-organ-and-carillon accompaniment played lustily.

Clarisse thrust her hands into her pockets and squeezed Valentine's wrists affectionately. "Got a blowtorch?" she whispered.

"I hate Christmas," he replied.

A strong gust dislodged a cherub and smashed it against the concrete a few feet from them.

"It's an omen," said Valentine.

"We'll have good luck for the rest of the year. Let's drink on it."

They hurried to the Café Vendôme on Commonwealth Avenue, which was mercifully out of sight of the Christmas tree. The small, intimately lighted café was uncrowded and warm, and they were so taken with the bartender, who didn't seem to be able to make up his mind between them, that they stayed through two rounds of Black Russians. When they made their way out onto the unpopulated boulevard of Commonwealth they did not mind the increasingly sharp gusts of wind.

As they neared Berkeley Street, Clarisse abruptly stopped and grabbed Valentine's arm. She nodded to direct his attention across the street, and as she did so she stepped back a few feet into the shadows. Retreating also, Valentine saw nothing more than a battered blue Fairlane, probably ten years old, maneuvering into a parking space. Its front fender was an incongruous bottle green.

"What are you pointing at?"

"The car," said Clarisse in a low voice.

"Who's in it?"

"Wait and see."

A tall man wearing a denim jacket opened the driver's door, and as he did so the interior light came on. He reached over into the backseat and retrieved a steering wheel lock, which with some difficulty he placed around the brake and wheel. He snapped down three locks on the doors, and climbed out of the car.

When Valentine saw the black sweater beneath the denim jacket he knew that it was the man who had sat beside him in the bar.

"What was his name?" he demanded.

"Hougan. Frank Hougan."

Hougan pulled a key ring from his back left pocket as he slid between the front of his car and the back of a painted van. He crossed the sidewalk, and leapt up the dozen steps of a narrow five-story town house. They watched him enter.

"That's his house?" said Valentine.

Clarisse nodded. "I have that house, and the one next to it. Eighteen flats in all. It's more—" She broke off, and pointed upward.

Valentine looked at the third floor. There, lights suddenly blazed on in two of the windows. After a moment Hougan passed in front of one of them and dropped his jacket to the floor. He disappeared. In another second, the third window was dimly lighted, and then became black again. Evidently he had opened a connecting door, so that light from the living room shone through, and then he had closed it again.

Valentine laughed. "I can see the beams."

"Yes," said Clarisse, "and it's a funny thing. There's no reason for them to be there. No structural reason, I mean. They're nowhere else in the building, and they certainly aren't original. Somebody who had the place before liked beams, I guess, and put them in."

"Where do you suppose Boots is tonight?"

"What do you mean?"

"Lights were out when he got home. He was probably looking in the bedroom for her, that's probably why he opened the door."

"I imagine she was in there asleep. It doesn't matter what time you call over there, you're bound to wake up Boots. Noon, three o'clock in the afternoon, eight o'clock in the evening."

"You sleep late too sometimes."

"At least I don't go to sleep *and* wake up stoned."

"How do you wake up stoned?"

"Ask Boots," said Clarisse. "I'm cold."

She pulled him on, in the direction of her own apartment, but Valentine jerked her back into the obscuring shadow.

Clarisse started to protest but Valentine touched his hand to her mouth. She was silent.

He pointed at a tall man moving toward them down the center of the boulevard. He proceeded in and out of the black shadows of the massive trees. Sometimes the lights of turning cars flashed over his flapping coattails, but his downturned face remained hidden.

Valentine backed tensely from the sidewalk onto the frozen mud of the boulevard. He dragged Clarisse with him. He relaxed a little when the man veered away from them, crossed the expanse of beaten dead grass, and stepped into the street. A car blew its horn at him, but he was oblivious to it, and by the time it had passed he was already marching down the sidewalk. He went up the steps of the same building Frank Hougan had entered. He stepped into the vestibule, and without hesitation, pushed a button there. In a moment, Clarisse and Valentine could see that he was buzzed in.

"Searcy?" said Clarisse.

Valentine nodded. "The walk gives him away. Arrogant. He could have a sex change, plastic surgery, and a new wardrobe by Diane Von Furstenberg and I'd still know him by his walk."

"You think he went in to see Hougan?" asked Clarisse. She looked back toward the building, and pointed. The light in the bedroom had come on.

"Boots *was* in there asleep," said Valentine.

"And the buzzer woke her up. I wish," continued Clarisse, "that we were on a level with those windows so that we could see what was going on. We can't see a damn thing unless somebody in there is practically leaning out over the ledge." She glanced behind her at the building directly across the boulevard. "We couldn't see anything from there anyway, trees are too thick I think."

"Why do you suppose Searcy is going to see somebody like Hougan?"

"Maybe he's answering the ad," said Clarisse lightly.

"Maybe he's on the vice squad."

"No," said Clarisse after a pause. "Hougan knew Searcy was coming. That's why he looked so funny when you mentioned Searcy's name this evening in the bar. That's why he left." Valentine nodded thoughtfully. "But the question is: what is Searcy doing, going to see somebody like Hougan?"

"That's what I just said."

Clarisse withdrew her hands from her pockets, and opened the leather envelope that she had carried all the while beneath her arm. "How'd you like to get a better angle on what's happening in that room?" She rummaged through her envelope, and handed Valentine a thick sheaf of dog-eared papers.

"There's no better angle. If we moved down the block, we couldn't see anything at all."

Clarisse triumphantly extracted a large ring of keys from the envelope. A tube of lipstick fell to the ground. Valentine leaned down, picked it up, and thrust it back into the envelope.

"What are you going to do?" he demanded.

"Something illegal and rude."

"What?"

"We're going inside. I've got the keys to the building. I was showing a place in the building next to it to two sweet little boys from Ohio yesterday, and they were pretending that they weren't gay, talking about their girlfriends and so forth, they probably thought we wouldn't rent to faggots—and as if they could fool me!"

Valentine gestured impatiently.

"Anyway, I had the keys, and it was cold and too far to walk back to the office, so I just kept 'em. So now all we have to do—"

"—is go in there, and walk up to the third floor, and knock on Hougan's door, and say 'Hi! We were just in the neighborhood and stopped by to see if your plumbing was OK!'?"

"No," said Clarisse sternly, "that would be silly. We go into the building next to theirs." She pointed to the third floor of the adjacent building. There, the windows of the flat next to Hougan's were dark.

Valentine eyed her dubiously. "That apartment's empty? That's the apartment you were showing to the little boys from Ohio yesterday?"

Clarisse nodded, after a moment of hesitation. "It belonged to the two Michaels and they moved to Newport."

"You think we can hear through the wall?"

Clarisse shrugged. "We can try. Valentine, aren't you curious? Don't you want to know?"

"Yes," he nodded, reluctantly, and followed her across the boulevard. They said nothing as they waited for the light at the corner to change. They hurried across the street and up to the door of the house. Clarisse tried six keys before she found the one that admitted them. "Someday I guess I really ought to label these keys. When you have more than about thirty, it's hard to remember which goes where."

They climbed quickly and silently to the third floor. They stopped nervously in the hall. Valentine listened intently while

Clarisse hunted for the key to the apartment. At last she found it, and unlocked the door.

She turned the knob, but held the door closed. "Take a deep breath," she cautioned him.

She flicked the light switch and opened the door on a completely furnished and inhabited-looking apartment.

"Jesus," cried Valentine, "it's a Neapolitan bordello!"

The small square room was covered in sea-green flocked wallpaper and had three large sofas upholstered in green plush velvet. The veneered end tables groaned beneath large crystal lamps with gold-fringed green damask shades. The curtains were of thickly lined gold silk, and behind them were shirred Austrian drapes. The floor was wall-to-walled in deep-pile gold carpeting. Directly beneath the three-foot gilt-and-crystal chandelier—the ceiling was only eight feet high—was a glass-topped coffee table on a brass base. On one corner was a collection of crystal frogs and on the other a stack of *Architectural Digests*.

"Clarisse," said Valentine severely, "this isn't what I'd call an empty apartment. Who the hell lives here?" His voice suddenly dropped to a whisper. "What if they're in the bedroom?"

"The two Michaels—nice Italian boys. One of them is very pretty, and one of them has a lot of money."

"And neither of them has any taste. But where the hell are they?" demanded Valentine.

"Providence. They were here yesterday when I showed the apartment—the two little boys from Ohio nearly fainted when I opened the door. You can't get this kind of furniture in Ohio, I bet. Anyway, the two Michaels said they were going down to Providence tonight to see a new production of *Uncle Tom's Cabin* at the Trinity Square Rep. The Topsy is supposed to be a scream. They asked the two little boys from Ohio to go with them. They probably won't be back for another hour or so."

"God, Clarisse, what if the production is awful, and they leave before it's over? What if they came in right now?"

"They won't. I've heard that the production is very fine. And probably they'll go to the bars afterwards. I hope."

Clarisse pushed open the bedroom door and snapped on the light. Though he was still nervous and muttering, "breaking and entering, breaking and entering," Valentine peered with fascination into the room. A low queen-sized bed with a chalk-white headboard and gilded finials took up most of the room. It was covered with a flocked black-and-brown spread in a lozenge design. Large white-and-gold bedside tables, of the same design as the end tables in the living room, bore lamps with high shades and crystal drops, while the bases were gold reproductions of Michelangelo's "David." The walls were robin's-egg blue, the taffeta curtains were canary yellow, and the carpet was scarlet. There was a gilt-framed mirror on the ceiling.

Valentine groaned.

"How do you have sex in a room like this?" asked Clarisse.

"With three Valiums and nerves of steel." Valentine collapsed on the edge of the bed, then suddenly stood, and straightened the material. From the nightstand nearer him he took a manual light dimmer and turned the dial, lowering the lights until the clashing colors were substantially muted.

Clarisse pulled her hair back, and pressed one ear against the wall, just to the side of a large gilt crucifix. "Hougan's bedroom is on the other side of this wall."

"I thought you said they had their flat soundproofed. How do you expect to hear anything?"

"Shhh."

Valentine moved about the room in short nervous steps.

Clarisse glanced at him and then hurried out of the room, motioning for him to remain. While she was gone, Valentine lowered the lights again.

Out of nervous curiosity, he opened the drawer of the bedside table, and to his delight, found a pack of cards, bearing on its reverse a photograph of the Monte Carlo casino. He riffled through the pack, extracted the joker, and slipped it into his jacket pocket. He put the pack at the back of the drawer, and pushed it closed with his knee.

Clarisse returned with a highball glass, with a gilt gothic-letter *M* engraved on the side. She placed the glass against the wall, base down, and pressed her ear within the mouth. Her face contorted with concentration.

She brightened almost immediately. "Moaning..."

Valentine moved over. Clarisse backed away, and Valentine placed his ear in the glass.

"Did you hear the whip?" whispered Clarisse.

"Sounds like a radiator to me. We're not going to be able to hear anything through a glass, Clarisse."

"Maybe we've got it backwards, and it's the *open* end that should go against the wall."

"No, I don't know. But this is a fire wall, and it's much too thick to hear anything through."

Clarisse shrugged, pulled back the heavy flocked drapes and unlatched the window.

"Maybe," she said, "maybe somebody threw the radiator against the wall."

"What the hell are you doing?"

Frigid air blew through the room as Clarisse raised the window high. She lifted one leg onto the sill.

"Do you want a push?" said Valentine.

Clarisse turned. "I want to get a look in there. There's a fire escape here that goes across both buildings. If they leave the curtains open in front, they probably leave 'em open in the back too." She tossed her leather envelope to Valentine.

"I think we ought to get out of here! I think you are out—"

Clarisse was gone. Valentine moved to the corner of the room beside the open window, so that he would be out of the way of the drafts. He took out a package of cigarettes, but glancing around the room, saw that there was no ashtray. He replaced the pack and picked up the Boston white pages from the bottom of the night table. He memorized the number of Randy Harmon's ex-lover Cal, the trial lawyer. He rubbed the cover of the book against his pants to destroy his fingerprints.

Clarisse's legs were pointed through the window. Valentine reached an arm through and pulled her in. Her face was red and her eyes glistened. Her breath came shortly, almost in sobs.

"Are they after us?"

She shook her head convulsively, and leaned heavily against the wall.

Valentine closed the window, latched it, and drew the drapes. "What'd you see?" he demanded.

"Let's get out of here. The two Michaels will be back any minute."

Valentine nodded. He pushed Clarisse out into the living room, flicked out the light and pulled the door shut. In another moment, they were out in the hallway, moving toward the stairs.

"What'd you see?"

"Don't ask," said Clarisse darkly.

They were on a landing, and Valentine pushed her against the wall. "What'd you see?" he demanded sternly. "Were the curtains open?"

She nodded. "I hunched against the bricks and looked in."

"Did they see you?"

She moved down the stairs, and whispered to Valentine over her shoulder. "No, they were busy..."

"Whips and chains?"

"Talk about wall hangings. You can see why Hougan wanted those beams."

"Somebody was hanging from the ceiling?"

Clarisse wasn't to be rushed into this. "They were doing it by candlelight, so I didn't see everything, and I couldn't look directly in, because they would have seen me..."

"Who was hanging from the ceiling?"

"Well, Hougan had on some sort of leather contraption, all straps and buckles and studs..."

"Was Boots there?"

"Valentine," said Clarisse, "Boots has a figure like a pair of Dixie cups nailed on a two-by-four. All black leather and spiked heels."

"What about Searcy?"

"Val," she said excitedly, as she pushed open the door into the vestibule, "did you put that glass back in the kitchen?"

"No," he said, unperturbed, "it's still in the bedroom, and it's got our fingerprints all over it. Not to mention the doorknobs and the light switches. Are your prints on file anywhere?"

"Not that I know of." Clarisse paused, with the door open. "Oh well," she said, "the two Michaels aren't the type to prosecute anyway."

Valentine followed her out into the cold. "What about Searcy?" he hissed.

"Better looking with his clothes off than on. Real definition. But Hougan certainly isn't, I'm sure that man doesn't work out. He ought to join—"

"What? Searcy already had his clothes off?"

"No. He was wearing chaps, black leather chaps..."

"And?"

"And nothing else."

"Was he..."

"He was getting there," said Clarisse. "Now this is embarrassing me, Val, and I don't want to talk about it anymore."

"Embarrassed? You drag me into someone's apartment in the middle of the night, and we're liable to be caught and prosecuted, and then you crawl out on a third-floor fire escape when the windchill factor is twenty below and stare in somebody's window, and you tell me you're embarrassed?"

"I'm not going to say another word. If you weren't so lily-livered and had come out on the fire escape with me, you would have seen everything yourself."

"We're going back to the Vendôme, and you're going to tell me everything you saw."

"You're paying," she said, "and I get the bartender."

"I'm paying," he said.

Half an hour later, Valentine had got all the details and a date with the bartender. Before parting, Valentine and Clarisse decided to walk once more past Hougan's building to see if the lights were still burning, and if the blue Fairlane were still there.

They stood at the edge of the boulevard, in the light of a streetlamp, and stared up at the lighted windows of Hougan's apartment.

The door of the building opened and Searcy appeared at the top of the stairs.

In one swift graceful movement Clarisse dropped her cigarette, and threw her arm over Valentine's shoulder. Her coat falling open obscured both their bodies, and she pressed her mouth hard over his. Her thick black hair covered both their faces from the policeman's sight.

Biting at Clarisse's tongue with playful malevolence, Valentine peered through her black hair at Searcy descending the steps. The man hailed a taxi.

Clarisse and Valentine held the embrace. "Tremont and Boylston," they heard Searcy say to the driver, and listened with relief to the slamming of the vehicle's door.

Clarisse pushed Valentine violently away from her. "Beast!" she cried.

Valentine leaned against a tree trunk and gasped dramatically for breath.

"Forty-five minutes, wouldn't you say?" said Clarisse, staring up at Hougan's window.

Valentine stood beside her. "When you're playing with toys, forty-five minutes is just a quickie."

"Maybe forty-five minutes is all a cop can afford."

"He's got enough to take taxis."

"Here to Tremont and Boylston won't cost him more than two dollars, with tip," said Clarisse. "Probably he just parked over there."

"Or maybe he's going to Nexus."

"Why? You think he's interested in little boys? Christ, Val, the man just did a performance with the Lunt and Fontanne of the leather set."

"No," said Valentine. "I don't think he's interested in little boys, but if he's into humiliation, getting worked over by a pair like Hougan and Slater, he's probably also into aggression. He's probably feeling like shit now, and he's probably on his way over there to take it out on somebody."

"That's the cheapest psychology I've heard since the Happy Hooker told Dinah Shore why she was so damned cheerful."

"Look, Clarisse, I don't want Searcy over there messing with Mack. It's too easy for a cop to threaten an ex-con."

"Is Mack one of yours?"

Valentine nodded. "He was in Charles Street for five-to-seven. Part of a car theft ring. Out of the whole gang, he was the only one caught and sentenced. He was in charge of painting the cars. I got him furloughed once a week to take the bartending course at Harvard, and then when he was released, I got him the job at Nexus. I thought he'd move on to a straight bar, but he says he likes it there. Mack's one of my success stories."

"Into the breach then! You throw yourself in front of Mack, and I'll hold Searcy off with a can of Mace and a cattle prod!"

"When you were out on that fire escape—"

"What?" demanded Clarisse.

"I should have locked the window."

Chapter Twelve

SEARCY'S TAXI LET him off at the Trailways terminal. He walked, a little unsteadily, through the parking lot, craning his head to make sure that his unmarked car hadn't been stolen from its place on Carver Street. The half a joint he'd smoked left him depressed and uncoordinated; he wondered sullenly if it had been treated with something.

As he approached his car, he had his keys out of his pocket. But with his hand on the door, he changed his mind, thrust the keys back into his pocket, and hurried past Herbie's Ramrod Room up to Tremont Street. He turned in the direction of the Combat Zone and Nexus.

Searcy was angry, with himself and with the entire confused investigation. For an insignificant teenager, who probably wasn't any colder in his grave than he would be on the streets tonight, William A. Golacinsky certainly had caused the police force a great deal of trouble.

The papers had by no means downplayed the murder, and this was certainly because of Scarpetti's involvement in the case. The representative, in a muddleheaded way that was characteristic of his entire life, public and private, had not yet determined for himself whether it was a good thing or a bad that little Billy's corpse had been discovered beneath his hemlocks. In general, corpses of hustlers couldn't help but be an embarrassment when they were strewn over the landscape, but Scarpetti dimly reckoned that he might turn the circumstance to his political advantage. He decided to take it as a personal affront. He first accused the homosexual community of murdering one of their number, and leaving the corpse upon his lawn in order to discredit him. There was a homosexual in his very neighborhood, he said indignantly, who might well have engineered the entire thing. He had also hinted that liberal legislators in the House had stolen the body from the morgue and planted it in retaliation against his having worked to defeat so many of their precious bills. He even dug in a little at Mr. Golacinsky himself, just in case it turned out that the teenager had committed suicide in obscure protest.

Because his mind was entirely fastened to the notion of putting the corpse to account, Scarpetti had been surprised by the attacks that had been leveled against him. *The Gay Community News* and *Esplanade*, the weekly gay newspapers in Boston, published extensive accounts of the crime on Wednesday, and included long interviews with mindless hustlers who had known Golacinsky. The papers suggested that some zealous adherents to Mr. Scarpetti's political beliefs had run out, murdered a hustler in an excess of admiration, and brought the corpse to Scarpetti's doorstep, as it were—rather after the fashion of a faithful but stupid dog that kills rodents and lays them as devoted offerings at the foot of its master's bed. The daily papers, on their editorial pages on Thursday morning, had reprinted these speculations without comment.

Scarpetti suddenly found himself on the defensive, and was very angry. Thursday noon, he made a personal appearance at District 2. Searcy missed that scene, but the effects were brought home to him by his immediate supervisor. Scarpetti wanted an arrest; he didn't care how unlikely the suspect was, so long as the murder could be pinned on somebody. If the jerk was innocent, then he'd get off; but it was essential that Scarpetti be exonerated, and that would only come with somebody's being brought in for murder. It would be very convenient, Searcy was given to understand, if the suspect were homosexual.

Searcy turned into Nexus and walked down the ramp with determined heavy steps. He pushed his way through the two dozen dancing couples beneath the whirling glitter ball. The swimming pinpoints of white and yellow lights broke across his eyes, and he tried to brush them away as if they had been gnats.

Searcy took the stool he had had two nights before, the stool on which Golacinsky had sat the night he was murdered.

Mack spotted him from the opposite end of the bar and crossed down smiling. "You thinking of becoming a regular here?" he asked in a friendly voice.

"No," said Searcy curtly.

Mack raised his eyebrows warily. "Then you're on duty?"

Searcy looked back blankly. "I'm on my own time now, unofficial overtime, you might say. I came back to find out who the man was that Golacinsky left here with on Monday night."

"I told you everything I know," replied Mack. "I don't remember the man any better tonight than I did when I talked to you before."

"I think maybe that's a lie. I think maybe if you were in the right atmosphere, and in the right place, you could remember exactly what that man looked like and maybe you could dredge up his name and his address and his telephone number."

Mack said nothing for a moment, then remarked, "I think they must have shown Edward G. Robinson films at the training academy. If you want a drink, order it now because I'm busy. Thursday is the beginning of the weekend on this street." Without waiting for Searcy's reply, Mack poured bourbon into a glass, dropped in ice from too great a height so that the liquor splashed over the rim. He slid it down in front of the policeman. "It's on the house. And it's also the last."

Mack turned to go.

"Don't walk away from me!" cried Searcy, loudly enough to turn half a dozen heads.

Mack leaned forward over the bar, turned his head slowly until he faced Searcy, and then hissed, "*Listen.* I cooperated with you down the line. I told you everything I know. I could tell you some other things but I'd be making them up. Now you come in here and threaten to drag me in to Berkeley Street. That's not good for my business, and you drag me in you'll find that it's not so good for your business either. When you're on duty, I'll listen to you, but right now you're just another customer."

Searcy took a pack of cigarettes from his jacket, extracted one and tapped it on the bar. "You've seen the movies, haven't you?" He lit the cigarette. "You watch television? You've heard of 'withholding evidence' and 'suspicion of being an accomplice'?"

"Your line's getting old, Lieutenant. You pulled that one on Randy Harmon last night. Didn't work then, won't work now."

Searcy drew hard on the cigarette. "News gets around this neighborhood fast. Do the fags have a community newsletter?"

"Yes, and in today's issue there's a warning against a nasty cop with curly hair and a drinking problem."

Mack moved down the bar, and resumed waiting on customers. Searcy fumbled with his cigarette and it fell to the floor. He lit another. Glancing over the dance floor, he saw Daisy Mae sidling toward him. She was smiling slyly, but seeing his expression, she pivoted and disappeared into the crowd.

Searcy took a swallow of his drink and looked toward the entrance.

Daniel Valentine and Clarisse Lovelace, shivering with cold, stepped into the light. They made their way down the ramp without even glancing over the room. They nodded to Mack, crossed directly to the bar and seated themselves. Mack moved over and whispered to them a few seconds. Clarisse looked up over Valentine's shoulder and stared at Searcy, without expression. Valentine turned briefly also, then back to Mack. The bartender moved away to prepare them drinks.

Searcy stared at the couple through two long swallows of bourbon.

Two of the dancers on the floor separated suddenly. One disappeared into the men's room, and the other made his way over to Valentine and Clarisse.

"Hot enough for you?" said Randy Harmon, as he moved to stand between them. He leaned back against the bar and propped the heel of one boot on the brass rail. "And I'm not talking about the temperature." He jerked his head in Searcy's direction.

"We know," said Valentine.

"Oh, God," said Clarisse flatly, "I feel like Joan Crawford in *Rain*. The boys are going to start to break up the place."

"It won't be over you," said Valentine. "Not in here."

Searcy, as soon as Randy had joined Clarisse and Valentine, had dropped off his stool, and now approached them slowly. He stopped directly before them. Mack hovered a few feet down, behind the bar. No one said anything for several seconds.

"Well, well, well," said Searcy finally, "if it isn't Nancy Drew and the Hardy Boys."

"Are you on duty?" said Randy, looking Searcy directly in the eye.

Searcy wavered slightly, but said nothing.

"No," said Mack, "he's off." He set two Black Russians on the bar. He pulled a bottle of Miller Light out of the cooler, snapped off the cap, and put it at Randy's elbow. "Combat duty."

Valentine lifted his glass in a toast. "Here's to Representative Mario Scarpetti, recently deceased William A. Golacinsky, and Lieutenant William Initial Unknown Searcy, hustlers and victims all." Valentine took a swallow. Randy smiled. Clarisse opened her coat and pushed it back on her shoulders.

Searcy's eyes drifted over her body.

"Why do you hang out with these guys?" he demanded thickly. "Why don't you find a real man?"

Clarisse sighed. "I don't know who writes the dialogue for the Boston police," she said, turning to Randy and Valentine, "but he ought to be laid off." She turned back to Searcy. "Because I like men who do kinky things. Do you ever do kinky things, Lieutenant?" She smiled sweetly.

"No," said Searcy, "and I don't waste my time with fags either."

"Is this an official inquiry into the private lives of Boston real-estate agents?"

"I'm just curious," said Searcy, and smiled unexpectedly. "I'm curious about a lot of things."

"Like what?" said Valentine.

"Oh," said he, maintaining the smile and turning to Valentine, "like I think it's curious that you should just happen to see Golacinsky on the Block the night he's murdered, and that *you*," nodding to Randy, "should just happen to check Golacinsky into the baths and not remember what the man who was with him, and paid for him, looked like. And that your friend behind the bar there"—he waved in Mack's direction— "should just happen to see Golacinsky with the same man, and not remember anything about him except exactly what Harmon here remembers. I think that's real curious. But what really gets me is that the three of you just by chance should happen to be friends. None of you knew Golacinsky, and all three of you came across him that night." Searcy smiled at them all.

"It's a small world," said Valentine, shrugging.

"It's not that small. Golacinsky bounced off the three of you like he was a pinball that night."

"The gay community here is close knit, Lieutenant," said Randy, "if you're a bartender or work at the baths, you see just about everybody there is to see, at one time or another. Besides, Mack and I admitted that we knew Golacinsky, we just didn't know him well. It was only Valentine who didn't know him at all."

"I think you're all a little too close, a little too friendly. Real close, real friendly, and real suspicious."

Randy reached into his back pocket and pulled out his wallet. He flipped it open languidly and extracted a small card.

This he handed to Searcy. "It's my lawyer," he said dryly. "Talk to him about suspicion."

"Oh," said Valentine, "small world again. That's my lawyer too."

Behind the bar, Mack nodded and smiled.

"I'm surprised he's not here," said Searcy after a pause, "because he's going to have a lot of business real soon, defending the three of you." His voice was thick. He pointed an unsteady finger at Randy. "You *know* who Golacinsky was with that night at the baths, and I want him. You know him too," he cried, stabbing toward Mack. "And don't pull that crap about not seeing him. I don't believe it, and no judge in court is going to believe it either, and I don't care if you've got ten lawyers up there to defend you and five faggot doctors testifying that you suffer from loss of memory—"

His voice rose, and those nearby turned to watch. Valentine and Randy were perfectly still and remained expressionless. Clarisse rubbed slowly at a spot of liquor that had spilled on her pants. Mack stood behind them, a little to the side, and slowly wiped the bar with a white cloth.

"—and one of you"—his finger wavered—"is going to tell me who he was."

Randy blinked. "You touch me and you'll have an assault charge slapped on you faster than it takes a queen to spot a closet case."

Searcy's hand dropped.

"Ever hear of something called 'harassment'?" said Mack, from behind the bar.

Clarisse looked up. "Why don't you go out and hunt for clues?"

"There aren't any clues," cried Searcy savagely.

"What about the lipstick on Billy G's handkerchief?"

"What about it?"

"What color was it?"

"Red."

"There are four hundred shades of red when you're talking about lipstick, Lieutenant," said Clarisse. "Don't tell me that the crime lab couldn't come up with any better than 'red'! Did you see it?"

He nodded distractedly.

She lowered the Black Russian from her lips, turned and tilted her head so that her mouth was lighted by a small white spot from above the bar. "Was it this shade?"

"Are you in on this too?" cried Searcy.

"Was it this color?" said Clarisse, still with her lips pouted in the light.

"Yeah, that color," said Searcy, "but a little darker."

"This is cerise, not red."

"Why? What does it matter?" said Searcy.

Clarisse shrugged. "I just wanted to know what shade was fashionable with murderers these days."

Searcy reddened.

"Go home and take a couple of Valium, Lieutenant. Get some rest," said Valentine solicitously. "Put some Vaseline on the rope burns."

"What!"

Clarisse turned and smiled. "*Frankly*, Lieutenant," she said, "how do you look in *Boots?*"

Valentine and Clarisse laughed. Searcy backed away. He staggered back to his stool, grabbed his coat, and rushed up the ramp.

Valentine and Clarisse turned languidly back to the bar. Randy and Mack looked at them in astonishment. "What was that all about?" Randy demanded.

"Just another runaround," said Valentine.

"The grapevine of wrath," said Clarisse.

"Did he bother you, Mack?" asked Valentine.

Mack shook his head. "Nothing I couldn't handle," he said proudly. "I don't know what you said to him, but I don't think it improved his temper."

"No," said Clarisse, "I don't think it did. But he'll think twice before he attacks one of us again."

"Spit it up," demanded Randy.

"It's Clarisse's story," said Valentine. "Brenda Starr on assignment couldn't have done it better."

Clarisse twisted about proudly on the stool. Then, at her request, Valentine related what had happened earlier in the evening. Clarisse smiled smugly.

Randy and Mack laughed with amazement throughout. "That takes care of Searcy," said Mack, and started to move away.

"Never underestimate a wounded straight man," cautioned Randy.

Valentine nodded. "You're right. Especially that one. We got rid of him tonight, but that's all the ammunition we've got. I'd be real surprised if he didn't come back. There's no—" He glanced at the clock behind the bar. "Oh, Christ! It's after twelve. Clarisse, we've got to run. I'm late for my divorce!"

Chapter Thirteen

AFTER HAILING A TAXI outside Nexus, Valentine and Clarisse rode in silence to Clarisse's apartment building on Beacon Street in Back Bay. While Valentine tried to count the rounds of Black Russians he had ordered that evening, Clarisse rested her head groggily on his shoulder. The driver was a small man hunched down in the front seat; Valentine could not see him through the heavily scarred Plexiglas divider.

Clarisse was jarred by a sharp turn around the corner of the Public Garden. "What you think Searcy'll do now, Val?"

Valentine shrugged. "We'll talk about it in the morning. Go home and get some sleep. He won't do anything tonight."

"I still have to walk Veronica Lake." She stared out the window at the blocks of brick townhouses and seemed surprised when the taxi stopped before her own building. She kissed Valentine quickly and whispered, "Don't start anything tonight that has to be finished in New Hampshire. If there's any real problem, though, just send Mark over to me and I'll straighten him out."

"That's not his problem," said Valentine.

"You know what I mean."

"I'll call you in the morning."

"Good-night," she said, and climbed out of the cab, tucking her leather envelope beneath her arm. Closing the door behind her, she said loudly. "Call me at the office, I plan to be in by nine tomorrow."

Valentine laughed and pulled the door closed; he asked the driver to wait until she was safely inside the building.

Clarisse waved from the lighted vestibule. Valentine looked at his watch; it was already twenty minutes past midnight. Mark would be stationed by the entrance to the Eagle, hoping every time the door opened that it would be Valentine who had pulled the latch. Mark was the type who felt these small disappointments. "You know where the Eagle is?" asked Valentine of the cabbie.

There was a sudden movement in the front seat and the shadowy driver sat up abruptly. He turned and peered through the small window of the Plexiglas. He was a handsome Puerto Rican with a dusky complexion, short dark curly hair and a shaggy moustache. Light from a car at an intersection sparked on a diamond chip in his right earlobe. He grinned at Valentine.

"Aha," said the driver, "you take your girlfriend home, and then you go out and play?"

Valentine rolled his eyes, and sighed. "Do you know where the Eagle is? I'm meeting my shrink there."

"I was going there anyway myself," said the driver. "I get off duty at one. Tell you what, you pay me what the meter says and I turn it off. I give you a ride on the roof." The man reached a slender dark hand over and flipped off the meter.

"You mean 'on the house.'"

"Two thirty-five."

Valentine pushed three dollars through the small open window, and signaled that he wanted no change. The driver took the money, and stamped down hard on the accelerator. The car screamed forward through a yellow light that was turning red and the driver didn't put on brakes until he pulled up in front of the Eagle with a grinding squeal five minutes later.

"Jesus Christ!" said Valentine shakily. "You've still got an hour till last call."

"I don't like to have rush," said the driver. He turned back and grinned at Valentine. "We don't have to go in. I can take you home now. No charge."

"No," said Valentine breathlessly, "my shrink promised to bring me four hundred downs tonight." He crawled out of the cab.

"See you in a minute," said the driver. By the time that Valentine had stepped the two feet to the curb, the taxi had screeched halfway down the block and was parking in a too-small space by the bumper-bashing method.

Valentine went through the open door of the bar with half a dozen other men; it was the most fashionable time for making an entrance. He jumped possessively onto an empty stool at the bar nearest the entrance, and ordered a rye, straight up. He gulped half of it down and looked cautiously behind him; Mark was not nearby. Valentine began to search further afield, holding the glass of rye to his lips.

The Eagle, Boston's largest leather-and-denim bar, had expanded steadily since its establishment two years before. The main bar was a square with fifty-foot sides; the walls were dark and not much altered or improved since it had been an establishment catering to after-game fans from Fenway Park. Along one wall was a badly executed mural depicting Custer's meeting with the Indians, that everyone wished would be painted over. Two swinging Plexiglas doors in the wall opposite the entrance led into the disco room. The lighting was dim, but high enough for good cruising. The pool table in the center of the floor had a plywood cover, and several men perched there now. On Thursday night, this part of the bar had a good crowd—about a hundred men—though this was not a third or even a fourth of the number that would be present on Friday and Saturday nights at the same hour.

The jukebox was pushed to highest volume to compete with the thumping disco music in the dance-bar. The dark leather and denim clothing of the men who stood about in small groups talking in low deep voices seemed to augment the shadows in the room. The pinball machines in the back glowed vibrantly in yellow and red, their bells ringing constantly as serious players shook and tilted them violently.

The cabdriver who had brought Valentine entered, and touched him lightly on the shoulder, smiling. He moved directly to the disco room.

Valentine slid off the stool and filtered slowly through the crowd, nodding to friends and acquaintances. When he had satisfied himself that Mark was not in the main room, he shoved through one of the swinging doors into the disco bar.

This room was characterized as much by the heat as by the flashing multicolored lights and the strobes. It was ill-ventilated and full of smoke. Though no more crowded than the other bar, everything here was intensified: the music, the light, the heady smell of liquor, sweat, and poppers. Valentine edged his way to the dance floor: the men here didn't mind the heat at all, for it gave the narcissistic the chance to shed their shirts, and it gave others who were less exhibitionistic the opportunity to look at firmly muscled chests and arms in January.

The lighting above the dance floor was so spasmodic and dim through the climax of the newest Donna Summer recording that it was some time before Valentine saw Mark, gyrating in flickering slow motion beside the long wall of mirror. His flannel shirt was tied about his waist, and Valentine noted with satisfaction what felling trees could do for a man's torso. Sweat glistened on Mark's face and flailing arms.

It was with even greater difficulty that Valentine picked out Mark's partner from the crowd of men near him, but finally he settled on a short Italian with curly dark hair, wearing an open denim work shirt and faded jeans. Valentine knew the record would go on for five more minutes and he would have that much time to formulate the kind words that would give Mark the permanent brush-off. He stared at Mark's chest and couldn't think of any words at all.

Turning to the bar, he ordered another rye and tried to concentrate on the problem at hand; but rather than Mark, his thoughts ran to William Searcy, Frank Hougan, Boots Slater, and William A. Golacinsky.

He wondered how Searcy had been caught up with Hougan. It did not seem possible that a man as uptight as Searcy—and one with a professional reputation to protect—would answer an ad in the *Phoenix* that talked about shackles and pain. It was more likely that Searcy had come across the couple in the line of duty. Golacinsky wasn't the first dead boy who had hung about the Block and the Block was only a few numbers down from Hougan's apartment; perhaps Hougan and Boots had been involved in another case. Searcy had given them the rough-cop routine, had found out from Boots, say, what the two got up to in the back room with the beams, and then had said something like, "Well, I ought to run the both of you in, but maybe we can work something out…"

What intrigued Valentine most, however, was that Searcy had taken part in the little games that Frank Hougan was playing up there on Commonwealth Avenue. It seemed impossible that a man as homophobic as Searcy could overcome his fear of his own attraction to men to allow Frank Hougan to come near him. On the other hand, it made a lot of sense that if Searcy were involved with any man sexually—even if it were in so peculiar a manner—it would be with a man like Hougan.

The Donna Summer ended and without allowing himself to think, Valentine hurried forward to catch at Mark. He and the short Italian had left the floor and stood in the farthest, darkest corner of the room. Mark was rebuttoning his shirt when Valentine came up before them.

"Oh, hi Daniel," said Mark, grinning sheepishly. "I'd almost thought you had decided to stand me up."

Valentine smiled and glanced at the shorter man. He had slipped his arm about Mark's waist, hooking his thumb into a belt loop. "I had to protect Clarisse against a roving band of dissatisfied apartment-dwellers. Introduce me."

"Oh, sorry," said Mark, evidently having hoped that Valentine would not ask. "This is Joseph."

Valentine and Joseph exchanged polite nods, and the silence that ensued would have been awkward had it not been overlaid with a hundred decibels of Grace Jones.

Joseph took a hint and unhooked his thumb. "Who wants a beer?" he asked, looking from Valentine to Mark. Valentine held his glass up to show that he was set.

"A Busch," said Mark, and Joseph moved off toward the bar. Valentine smiled at Mark, without the least idea in the world of what he was going to say.

"You're not upset, are you?" asked Mark, biting his lip in apprehension.

"Does it show?"

"Oh!" cried Mark, "I'm so sorry, Daniel. I know we had a date, but the music got to me, and Joseph asked me to dance, and—"

"I'm not upset about Joseph," interrupted Valentine, "something else entirely. Something that happened a while ago, something that doesn't have anything to do with you. In fact, I was coming here to tell you how glad I was that you came down to see me this weekend, and that nothing makes me happier than being able to give you a place to crash...Do you understand?" Valentine smiled and touched Mark's arm affectionately.

For a moment, Mark said nothing, thinking hard. Then he smiled. "I know," he said at last. "I guess I expected more, but I'm glad to see you again too. I guess when I was up in New Hampshire, I had some funny ideas. I was thinking about you all the time, I was always thinking about coming down here to see you in Boston..."

"You weren't thinking about me," said Valentine, "you were just thinking about *men*."

Mark nodded. "I guess so."

"I'll tell you something," said Valentine, "when you were down here last summer, I think I fell in love with you a little bit..." Even beneath the harsh red light that flooded them, Valentine thought he could detect a blush suffusing Mark's face.

"Oh yeah?" said Mark softly.

Valentine nodded. "But I'll tell you something else: bartenders make lousy husbands."

Mark laughed shortly. "I guess I knew that, and if I didn't, I should have. Is everybody from New Hampshire as much of a hick as I am?"

Valentine smiled, leaned forward and kissed Mark hard on the mouth. "Thanks for the jacket. It's going to mean an improvement in my love life." He glanced behind him and saw that Joseph was making his way back with two beers. "Has he asked you home yet?"

"Well, he wanted to, but—"

"He doesn't have a place?"

Mark shook his head. "He's in town for the weekend."

"Where's he from?"

Mark grinned. "New Hampshire..."

Valentine's eyebrows rose slowly.

"Laconia. About half an hour from me. He drives an oil truck."

"Good God," said Valentine. "Aren't there any faggot hair-dressers in New Hampshire?"

Mark thought a moment. "No," he said.

Joseph came up hesitantly. Valentine smiled at the small man warmly. "Mark, you have the keys to the flat. Crisco's under the sink, poppers are in the freezer." Joseph giggled.

"Got your rig outside?" said Valentine, turning to Joseph with a smile.

"No," said Joseph. "I came down in the pickup."

"A lumberjack and a truck driver in a pickup, and in my bed. It's so butch I can't stand it. You two get out of here."

"Daniel, we can't make you sleep on the sofa."

"You don't think I'm going to try to sleep while you two are going at it in the bedroom, do you? I can't sleep when I'm jealous. I'm going over to Clarisse's."

"Oh," said Mark, "that's really inconveniencing you, though. I can't—"

"Yes you can," said Valentine sharply. "I couldn't live with myself if I thought I was keeping you two apart. Besides, Clarisse likes to wake up with a man in her flat."

Mark leaned forward and embraced Valentine warmly. In Valentine's ear he whispered, "No wonder I'm in love with you."

Valentine broke the embrace. "Have a good time. Come and go as you like. I have an extra set of keys." He pushed away into the crowd.

In the darkness at the edge of the dance floor, he was grabbed. The taxi driver had him fast by both arms. "No shrink. You leave your girlfriend for a threesome..."

"No group therapy for me," laughed Valentine, "at least not tonight. But I could be up for a little one-to-one."

"You want a ride to my place, then?"

"Sure," said Valentine, "for an hour or two anyway. Then I got to get back to my girl, she's so lonesome without me."

Friday, 5 January

Chapter Fourteen

"GOD," MOANED Clarisse as she buried her face in her hands. Her elbows propped on the table began to slip forward. "I could kill you for pushing those Black Russians on me, Val." She looked up suddenly, tossing her hair back from her face. "You don't look particularly hung over," she said accusingly. "What time did you come in?"

Valentine sat on the other side of the small walnut table that was nestled in the bay window of Clarisse's apartment. A few inches from them, on the other side of the glass, the morning was cold and bleak. Slate-gray clouds billowing across the sky threatened more snow and a steady frigid wind blew down Beacon Street. The limestone townhouses across the way, housing for the students of a junior college, were a lifeless and depressing backdrop.

"I got in at three. I'd have been in earlier but I had a run-in with a taxi driver. And I don't have a hangover because I took two aspirin before I went to sleep. And you needn't envy me because I paid my dues last night sleeping on your Castro Convertible rock."

"Don't blame me. My bed sleeps two." She looked askance at the cup of coffee that he poured for her and pushed across the table. She took a deep breath, grimaced and pushed it away, and then leaned back in the cane chair. She crossed her legs and rearranged the flaps of her rust-colored velour robe. She glanced at the coffee cup again, picked it up, waved it beneath her nose, and set it back down on the table.

"Yeah," said Valentine, slow on the uptake, "you and Veronica Lake."

At the sound of her name, the tawny afghan padded eagerly into the living room and nuzzled against Clarisse's thigh. Clarisse ran her fingers through the dog's silky hair.

"Good girl," Clarisse said, "go shed on Valentine."

Valentine had moved to the sofa with his coffee. Veronica Lake obediently went over to him and thrust her head familiarly into his crotch.

"You teaching her tricks?" said Valentine.

"She's a natural," said Clarisse. "I took her out last night when I got in, and we went past Hougan's place. The car was still there, but the lights were out in front. They may have been in the back entertaining another guest, but the alley behind Commonwealth is dangerous at night, so I didn't go back there. Anyway, Veronica Lake ought to be ready to go out again—I don't understand why she's being so calm."

"I took her out when I got up."

"Good God," said Clarisse, "you took out the dog, fixed real coffee, made the bed. As long as you're playing domestic, why don't you get me a couple of aspirin?"

Valentine rose and went into the bathroom. In a moment he returned with his hand outstretched. Clarisse took the aspirin. "God," she breathed, "I forgot to call in sick."

"I did that too," said Valentine.

"Thanks. What'd you tell them?"

"That you had yellow eyes and it was either malaria or hepatitis, the doctor didn't know for sure which yet. How well do you know Boots?"

"Boots?" She looked vaguely under the table at her bare feet.

Valentine sighed. "Miss Lash LaRue. How well do you know her?"

"I don't know anything more than what I've told you."

"We've got to talk to her."

"About what?"

"Searcy."

Grimly, Clarisse swallowed the aspirin with a long gulp of coffee. She looked to Valentine to continue.

"At first," he said, "I thought he was just another homophobic cop on a routine investigation. But now I think there's something else."

"Sure, the games that he likes to play with Boots and Hougan."

"No, not just that. That's interesting, sure, but that's not much more than good gossip. In case you didn't notice, I also bought the paper this morning. Scarpetti told the *Globe* that the police have narrowed their investigation to within the gay community, or as he puts it, 'the homosexual underground'—as if the light of day injured our eyes..."

"Hurts mine," piped Clarisse.

"They don't know it was a fag that did it," said Valentine, ignoring her interruption, "that's just what they want to think. So Searcy is pushing hard. He pushed on Randy Harmon, he pushed on Mack, he's starting to push on me a little too, I think. I want to know why because I want to be able to stop him if he starts to come down any harder. None of us killed that little boy but Searcy might be able to pull out an indictment somewhere. I don't intend to stand around and let myself and my friends get victimized."

"I think that little bomb we dropped on him last night should slow him up for a bit."

"I don't," said Valentine. "That's why we've got to talk to Boots."

"You mean that's why *I've* got to talk to Boots, right?"

Valentine nodded.

"Sure," Clarisse shrugged. "But why exactly?"

"I don't know, just talk to her. Maybe it'll help."

"All right," said Clarisse, a little less groggily now that she was drinking her coffee, "but how do I go about this? Stiff-arm my way in, and scream, 'All right Slater, we've got the goods—come clean or it'll go hard with you!'?"

"Maybe something more subtle," said Valentine.

Clarisse stared out the window a few moments. Then she turned back to Valentine. "Phone book," she demanded.

Valentine reached over the back of the sofa for the Boston white pages.

"No," said Clarisse, "my own book."

Valentine swerved and snatched the thick dog-eared black leather book from the end table, and carried it with the telephone to the table by the window. He returned to the sofa.

Clarisse turned the pages of her book rapidly, apparently not able to find the number she wanted.

"Slater," suggested Valentine, "or Hougan."

"No," said Clarisse, squinting in concentration. "*Remembrance!*" She quickly flipped the pages.

"Remembrance?"

"Of things past. I'm calling Marcel."

"He's dead."

"Not Marcel Proust. Marcel *Wave*. Du Côté Chez Marcel. I'm calling Raymond."

Valentine turned away in disgust. "Look, your hair can wait, OK? Why don't you call Boots?"

Clarisse ignored him and dialed. She fought a yawn just as a female voice on the line intoned: "Du Côté de Chez Marcel." The accent was less French than Flatbush. "Ici Albertine."

"Raymond Craven please," said Clarisse in her smoothest voice.

"Pardon?"

"Swann," replied Clarisse reluctantly.

"Mais certainement, madame." The line clicked to hold.

"Swann?" said Valentine skeptically.

"They've all got professional names. Get your hair shampooed by the Baron de Charlus, and your nails trimmed by the Duchesse de Guermantes."

"Cute," said Valentine, "real cute."

Clarisse uncupped the receiver when a male voice came on. "Oui, ici Swann."

"Raymond, this is Clarisse Lovelace."

There was a slight pause as the accent was dropped. "Hi, Clarisse."

"Raymond, listen, I need a favor—a big one."

"Sure. I owe it to you. You got an enemy you want hennaed to death?"

"Why do you owe me?"

"You got my landlord to put in new tile in the bathroom and kitchen without raising the rent."

"Good," said Clarisse. "I'm calling in the favor. Can you do two heads at once?"

"At the same time?"

"No, but during the same hour?"

"Yes, sure."

"Two for one o'clock this afternoon?"

Raymond paused: "That's my break, Clarisse, and I didn't have any dinner last night. Nobody stays around this place at one except Albertine."

"Please, Raymond!" cried Clarisse desperately. "I'll bring you a two-inch slab of pâté en croute and a quart of Perrier. I wouldn't ask except that it's just the most important thing in the world! I have this friend and she needs a really good cut, and she's awfully shy. She's been a Carmelite for the past eight years and she just left the order three weeks ago and she's never had her hair cut professionally before and it's just a mess. Tonight she's got a hot date with that cute man who works at the charcuterie in Quincy Market—you know the one I mean, the one that you're in love with except that he's straight—and I told her that she wouldn't get to first base with him unless she got Swann to do her hair."

"Why does it have to be at one? Why can't you just schedule her in the regular way?"

"Oh," cried Clarisse, turning in the chair to avoid Valentine's glare, "because, Raymond, she's so shy. She was a nun—you know how shy nuns are, especially ex-nuns. You saw *The Nun's Story*. She wouldn't be comfortable if there were a lot of women getting their hair cut at the same time, but if it's just me there, she'll be fine."

"Well," said Raymond, "I've never crimped a Carmelite before."

"Don't be irreverent. Listen, we could both use manicures too."

"No way. The Duchesse de Guermantes wouldn't give up lunch to do Patty P. Hearst's nails."

"Well," said Clarisse, balling her fists, "skip the manicure."

"Be here at one," said Raymond with a sigh.

"At one," said Clarisse. She hooked the receiver over her shoulder and broke the connection with her index finger. With her other hand she flipped forward through her phone book. "Don't say a word," she said to Valentine, "just give me your bandanna."

Valentine rose and stamped across the rug. He pulled his blue bandanna from his back pocket and threw it at her. Clarisse shook it open and draped it over the mouthpiece.

Valentine returned to the couch, and sat with folded arms, staring at Clarisse.

The line connected on a series of hacking coughs. Clarisse held the receiver away from her ear and rolled her eyes. When the coughing had subsided a soft female voice dragged out an unintelligible greeting that Clarisse took for "Hello?"

"Could I speak with Ms. Winifred Jean Slater please?" Clarisse asked in a low sophisticated voice.

"Who? Oh sure, yeah, that's me." Her voice was thin and whiney.

"This is Ms. Slater?"

"Uhhh, my name is Boots, that's right."

"Yes, well, Ms. Slater, I am pleased to inform you that you have been awarded a free shampoo and hair cut at Du Côté de Chez Marcel located at Number—"

A loud *clunk* sounded in Clarisse's ear as the telephone was dropped on the other end. After a moment filled with curses, the phone was recovered. "Wait a minute, lady," said Boots, "let me go into the other room."

Then, after the flushing of a toilet, the running of water from a faucet, spraying from an aerosol can, and soft stumbling footsteps, there was a small sigh. "OK, I'm back. I won something?"

Clarisse explained to Boots what she had won. "I tried to get hold of you for the past several days, Ms. Slater, but haven't been able to reach you. Your prize must be claimed at one o'clock this afternoon."

"Today?" asked Boots.

"Yes, dear. Doesn't this make you happy now?"

"Uhhh yes, I guess it does. Except that I don't need to get my hair cut. Is it one yet?"

"No, dear, you have plenty of time to get dressed and ready to go. I believe you live on Commonwealth Avenue between Berkeley and Clarendon? Well *Chez Marcel* is located only one block away, on Newbury Street, also between Berkeley and Clarendon. And Ms. Slater, this is a wonderful opportunity to have your hair done by a top French designer, Monsieur Swann, who just last week was chosen to style Julie Nixon Eisenhower's head."

"Oh yeah? Look, I don't know if—"

"Please do me a favor, Ms. Slater."

"What?"

"Examine a strand of your hair. Is it dull and lifeless? Lacking in body?"

"Uhhh...yeah, that's right. How'd you know?"

"Many women have this problem, Ms. Slater. And unless it is corrected in time, your hair may be permanently damaged. In six months it might be necessary to shave your head entirely. And how would you like that, Ms. Slater?"

"Well, you know, I've thought about it, but I don't think I'd like to have it done in winter. Maybe if—"

Clarisse grimaced and interrupted. "I forgot to mention one other thing, Ms. Slater. If you claim your prize this afternoon you will also qualify as a runner-up for an all-expenses-paid month-long vacation in sunny Puerto Rico. There are only nine other runners-up, so your chances are one in ten."

"Puerto Rico?"

"Think of being in Puerto Rico at this time of year!"

"Oh, yeah. I like Puerto Rico. I've been to Puerto Rico. Ummmm listen, I'm a little stoned, could you go through this again?"

Clarisse made a face, stuck out her tongue, struck her fist violently against the windowsill, and said politely, "Of course, I'd be happy to, dear."

Five minutes later she hung up, having extracted a promise from Boots Slater that she would be at Chez Marcel at one.

Clarisse neatly folded Valentine's bandanna, and brought it over to him on the sofa. Valentine shook his head, and said nothing.

After a quick shower and two more aspirins, Clarisse changed into a gray silk dress with wide padded shoulders, black seamed hose and matching gray heels. She replaced the thin gold chain about her neck with a silver one, and applied a fresh Band-Aid to the finger she had punctured on Veronica Lake's leash. She wore no makeup except for a slight blush on her cheeks.

"How do I look?" she said, turning before Valentine. "Chic enough for Newbury Street?"

"The butterfly's boots," he said languidly. "Why all the bother?"

Clarisse sat on the edge of the sofa and tightened a strap on one shoe. "I have to pick up my winter's supply of perfume today. If I go into Bonwit's dressed like this, that little twerp at the perfume counter will never dream of checking my account—I haven't paid a cent in four months." She took a cigarette from a pack on the coffee table and lit it. "Well, what kind of information do you want out of Boots?"

Chapter Fifteen

SITTING COMFORTABLY in a padded designer armchair, Clarisse Lovelace studied her reflected image. She tapped the ashes from her cigarette into a small porcelain ashtray on her crossed knee. Raymond pushed her head from one side to the other as he decided on the most flattering cut for her.

They were alone in Chez Marcel, except for Albertine, stationed well away from them, at the receptionist's desk by the front door. Speakers strategically placed around Raymond's dais at the back of the shop played quadraphonic Rameau.

Raymond left off knocking Clarisse's head about and caught her gaze in the mirror. Clarisse raised one eyebrow in question. He glanced at the ornate mantel clock on the marble fireplace behind them; it was chiming.

"Fifteen after one, Clarisse. Where's our nun?"

"She'll be here any minute," said Clarisse confidently.

He looked away. "Anyway, you don't need a full cut yet. Just a smart trim will do you."

"Whatever." She drew on her cigarette, and glanced nervously toward the front of the shop. She had a view of Newbury Street also but Boots was not in sight.

Raymond opened a cabinet under his counter and pulled out a nylon smock—sewn in imitation of the French flag—and tied it about Clarisse's neck.

She placed her ashtray on the armrest and stubbed out the cigarette. Raymond turned back to the counter and arranged his scissors and combs on a mirrored Art Deco tray. He glanced up at himself in the mirror absently, and ran a comb through his wavy brown hair. Then he took up a pair of tiny clippers and pricked at his moustache.

"Thanks for the pâté," he said, "but I wish you had brought Daniel instead."

"He's taking Veronica Lake for a run on the Common. I'll tell him you were asking when I see him later."

Raymond nodded and leaned closer to the mirror, turning his swarthy cheeks in the light to check for recent flaws.

"Monsieur Swann can have his facial later," said Clarisse.

"Sorry," he said, unapologetically, and stepped back behind her. With long strokes he quickly combed out her hair.

"Ummmm—" said Clarisse, but did not continue.

"Ummmm, what?"

"I have a confession to make, Raymond, I, ah—"

The opening bars of "The Marseillaise" chimed as the front door was opened. Both Clarisse and Raymond turned to watch Boots Slater stumble inside.

Raymond's hands dropped heavily onto Clarisse's shoulder. "*That*," he exclaimed quietly, "was a Carmelite?!"

Boots's motorcycle hat was pulled so far forward that her eyes were completely shadowed. Her tailored black leather jacket was zipped tight about her slender body, the collar turned up high. Her leather pants, with the heart in gold studs nestled in her crotch, outlined almost nonexistent hips and sinewy thighs. Her shiny black boots, thick-soled and heavy, were laced to the knees.

"I'm here about the trip to Puerto Rico," she whispered hoarsely, and struggled to remove her mirrored sunglasses.

Albertine turned with wide eyes, and stared at Raymond.

Raymond moved to the edge of the dais, and leaned forward. "She's all mine, Albertine." He motioned Boots over.

Raymond turned quickly back to Clarisse. Avoiding his glance, she was bending over the side of her chair and rummaging in her leather envelope for cigarettes. Raymond grabbed a chair and pushed it next to Clarisse, angling it toward the mirror. "So who is she, Sister Birgitta of the Apostolic Whip?" he hissed.

Boots crossed the front part of the shop unsteadily, and took her time mounting the two steps to the dais. She paused on the second step, both hands on the railing, and looked about.

She was in her late twenties, with a pale complexion that was only accented by her dark vague eyes and the pink rouge high on her cheeks. Her mouth was full and bright pink. For all the black severity of her outfit, Boots Slater had something about her of naïveté and innocence. After a few moments, her eyes alighted on Raymond, who had been staring at her intently. Clarisse had turned her chair so that her back was to Boots.

"Ms. Slater?" Raymond asked.

"Oh," she said thinly, "are you the man who's supposed to cut my hair so that I can get to Puerto Rico?"

"Yes, of course," he said, and snatched another French flag from his cabinet. "Won't you sit down, *s'il vous plaît.*" He waved her into the chair next to Clarisse's.

Boots took a deep breath, and walked toward the chair. She stared at it a moment while she drew off her gloves. She unzipped her jacket and sidled into the chair as if she were boarding a very small boat on a very turbulent sea. She folded her tiny hands into her narrow lap and stared blankly, and with something very like resignation, into the mirror.

Raymond fastened the French flag around her neck.

Clarisse suddenly sat up, cigarette in hand, and whirled around in the chair. "Do you have a light...?" She stopped, and surprise overspread her face. "Boots?" she cried.

Boots raised her eyebrows and turned slowly to Clarisse.

Clarisse bent forward, smiling warmly. "What a surprise to find you here! How have you been?"

"Hi," said Boots, with a smile that was friendly, but didn't show her teeth. "I've been great. How about you?"

"Oh, the usual. Do you have a light?"

"Oh, yeah." She fumbled under her smock, and Clarisse counted the number of buttons that got unsnapped. After the sixth, Boots's hand emerged with a pack of Marlboros. Beneath the cellophane on one side were four joints, and beneath the cellophane on the other was a folder of matches.

She took a cigarette for herself, and then lit both. Clarisse set the ashtray on the arm of her chair for them to share.

Boots looked hard at Clarisse. "Do I know you?"

Clarisse laughed and avoided Raymond's eyes in the mirror. Briefly, she reminded Boots who she was. Boots nodded and looked back to the mirror.

Raymond set his mouth, and then pulled off Boots's hat with a flourish. Straight dull brown hair fell to her shoulders. Raymond gathered it in both hands, and let it fall through his fingers. "You don't use a conditioner, do you?" he said tonelessly.

Boots shook her head.

"The human head has twenty thousand individual strands of hair. Nineteen thousand of yours have split ends. The best thing I can do for you, Ms. Slater, is give you a short cut." He looked at her hard in the mirror. "Something soft and feathery."

"Sure, I mean if Julie Nixon Eisenhower trusts you, why shouldn't I?"

Raymond turned to Clarisse's reflection and smiled blandly. "Why don't I cut Ms. Slater's hair first, Clarisse? That way she can be out of here quickly—and I'll have all the time in the world to do a job on you."

Clarisse shrugged uneasily.

Raymond took Boots briefly into the back room and shampooed her hair. When he led her back—she had evidently forgotten the way—Clarisse looked up from a pile of leases that she was reading through and smiled warmly at Boots.

Boots seated herself and lit another cigarette. Raymond combed her damp hair through.

"So how are things on Commonwealth, Boots?"

"Just great, ah—"

"Clarisse," smiled Clarisse. "My name is Clarisse. How's Frank?"

"Frank's really great. He sort of got pissed off when you made us put in soundproofing, but then the guys came over to do it, and he sort of got into watching them. You know, we'd get stoned and sit on the floor and watch these hot guys putting in soundproofing. It was great, you know?"

"Well," smiled Clarisse, "I'm glad all that worked out. That's a good building, but you've been having a lot of excitement in that neighborhood lately, haven't you?"

"You mean Frank and me?"

"No," said Clarisse, "on the Block."

Raymond paused, and glanced at Clarisse.

"Oh yeah," laughed Boots. "Frank calls the Block our backyard, except that it's really out in front, and it's down the street some."

"Why does he call it that?"

"'Cause he says there's nothing better than being able to work in your own backyard."

"You mean Frank works the Block?"

Boots didn't answer immediately. Her gaze wandered toward Raymond. Clarisse fished a moment for her meaning, but then reassured her. "Don't bother about Raymond. He's an ex-priest, and he's used to hearing confessions. He's never repeated a word of gossip in his life. Have you, Raymond?" She didn't wait for his reply before repeating the question to Boots. "You mean Frank works the Block?"

"Only when things are real slow. Sometimes our ad just gets completely ignored, and then the next week, half the North Shore calls in, and they all want to come by on the same night."

Raymond's clippers moved sluggishly through Boots's hair.

"How's business?" asked Clarisse. "Did you have a Christmas rush?"

"No, about the same as always." She brightened abruptly. "You have a boyfriend, don't you, Clarisse?"

"Not really."

"What about that man with the blond beard? He's real cute."

"Oh, you mean Valentine."

"That's a strange name. Is that a nickname? You know, Boots is a nickname too. It's not my real name."

"Valentine is his last name. You think he's cute?"

Boots nodded. She leaned a little closer to Clarisse. "Frank thinks he's cute too." She winked laboriously.

Clarisse took a long drag on her cigarette and flipped her hair to one side. "Does he?"

Boots pulled back. "Sure. Frank says he's hot." She turned suddenly to Raymond. "Can I take my jacket off, it's so hot in here?"

He lifted the smock and Boots wrestled out of her jacket. Beneath she wore a sleeveless rayon blouse. Plainly visible on her right shoulder was a series of four bruises in the yellow-green stage of healing. Clarisse stopped Raymond from lowering the smock, and ran her finger lightly over Boots's shoulder.

"What happened?"

Boots glanced at her shoulder and drew back. She covered the marks with one hand and pulled the smock over it. Raymond gave a two-beat pause and resumed clipping.

"What happened, Boots?"

Boots nervously lit another cigarette.

Clarisse touched Boots's arm gently. "Did Frank do that?"

Boots looked away a moment. "Yes," she answered blankly.

"Has he ever hit you before?"

"Yes."

"When did he do that to your shoulder?"

"New Year's," she replied immediately, then corrected herself. "No, Christmas. It didn't hurt, I just bruise easy."

"Do you have any other bruises now?"

Boots was silent and her eyes became moist. Raymond grabbed a handful of tissues from the counter and handed them to Boots. She dabbed at her eyes, and balled the damp tissue in her hand. She did not pull back when Clarisse laid a comforting hand atop hers.

"I didn't mean to upset you, Boots. I just hate to see any man treat a woman like that."

Boots nodded and unsnapped another button underneath her smock. She withdrew her hand and popped a yellow pill into her mouth. She swallowed it quickly.

"You have a headache?" asked Raymond.

"No," said Boots, "it was just a Quaalude."

They sat in silence for a while and soon Boots relaxed and sighed contentedly. "'Ludes are just great. They make everything all right. You want one, Clarisse?"

"Has that already begun to take effect?"

"No," said Boots, "but just knowing it'll hit makes me feel a lot better. And it works faster if you're already high. I got high before I came here you know. I don't like to leave the apartment unless I'm high, 'cause I might get in trouble or something."

"Listen, Boots, tell me something. When Frank works the Block, is he out there, well—looking for clients for both of you?"

Boots nodded. "Sure. You'd be surprised how many people really get into it—people right off the street. 'Course we get most of our people from the ad, or we get referrals sometimes too. We get people who have their names in the newspaper, and not for committing crimes either."

"You mean, like politicians?"

"Sort of."

"Sort of a politician?" said Clarisse. "You mean like, say, a policeman?"

"Yeah, that's right. We have this policeman, I can't tell you his name, we don't tell people's names. Most of 'em give false names anyway..." Boots's speech began to slow. She suddenly lost herself in contemplation of her reflection in the mirror. "What was I saying?"

"You were telling me about Lieutenant Searcy," said Clarissa boldly.

"Oh, yeah, but I wasn't supposed to tell you his name. You know him?"

"He's a good friend of mine these days. He said he knew you, and he had been over to your place a couple of times—"

"He didn't bust you for something, did he?"

"No," said Clarisse, "why do you say that?"

"'Cause that's how we met. Sometimes Bill works vice. Frank was down on the Block one night and Searcy came up to him and Frank made a proposition, you know, 'come back to my place and I'll show you my toys and we'll have a good time.' Frank can always tell when they're into toys."

Raymond's eyes widened. He folded his arms and slipped his scissors into his breast pocket.

"So Bill said he was the vice and he was going to take Frank in. And then Frank had to do some fast talking. Bill had had a few drinks, and Frank told him that the only reason he was out on the Block was so he could get enough money to pay off the doctor who let me have my last abortion. Bill said he didn't believe him, and then Frank said, 'Well come back to the apartment and I'll introduce you to Boots, and we can all sit down and have a drink, and Boots'll tell you about her abortion.' So they came back, and I played along about the abortion thing—I'm real good about playing along—and I made Bill a drink and then went in the bedroom and changed into my hot pants and came out with 'em unzipped and made Frank zip 'em up, and Frank said his fingernails were too short and made me go over to Bill and have him do it, and Frank went in the bathroom for about ten years and when he came out, Bill and I had already gone into the bedroom. I shut the door and took all my clothes off and told Bill that Frank was just on the Block trying to drum up business because he was a Vietnam vet and couldn't get a job, and that it was all right 'cause Frank lived with me and I'm a woman and what would Frank want with little boys when he's got me at home? You know what I mean?"

Clarisse nodded. "Then Bill isn't a client of yours. I mean he doesn't pay you? There are still some things he keeps secret from me."

Boots coughed during this question, and after clearing her throat, said "What?"

"I know he's been back. Does he pay you?"

"Well, sort of. How'd you know he came back?"

Clarisse didn't answer, and Boots went on. "It's sort of complicated. I mean he's a cop, so you just don't charge him the going rate. And he's got lots of problems, and every time he comes over he's got these mind games that he wants to play."

"Mind games?"

"Well, Bill kept coming back, and at first it was just me and him, and Frank would go out and get cigarettes, and then Bill wanted to play with toys and that was fine, because you know, that's kind of my specialty, and then he started wanting Frank to hang around and watch and Bill thought that he was humiliating Frank. So Frank sort of pretended that he was being humiliated, but actually Frank gets off on watching. Of course, I never told Bill that. But you know what all that means, don't you?"

"No," said Clarisse and Raymond at once.

"Well, sure," said Boots, "if Bill gets a kick out of having Frank watch, then somewhere in the back of his mind he wants to do it with Frank himself. It just all adds up, and so a few weeks ago when Bill came over and started on his mind games I got fed up, and I made him do it with Frank—and *I* watched."

"*You* made him?"

"Oh I'm real different when I'm working. I get into it, you know. Bill did it because it was part of the scene and he really got into it, but of course when it was over he got real mad and said he was going to run us both in. But we talked him out of it, saying he hadn't really had sex with Frank, it was really just part of having sex with me. So he kept on coming back, and he did it with Frank again—but only if I made him. I like that, because I got tired of doing all the work and especially when we weren't getting the full rate, and now Frank had to do part of it and I could sit back and watch. You know what I mean? You know, if you and Bill are getting it on these days, you ought to come over one night. We could all have a real good time. You got anything that's real shiny you could wear?"

Before Clarisse could answer, Boots had turned to check her reflection. "Is that it?" she said to Raymond. "I mean, won't it look kind of funny so short on one side, and real long on the other?"

Raymond pulled the scissors out of his breast pocket and continued the cutting.

"Well," said Clarisse, "things really *are* busy in your neighborhood, what with Searcy and that little hustler that got murdered this week."

"You mean what's-his-name?"

Clarisse looked at her for a long moment. "You knew him then? His name was Billy Golacinsky."

"No, I read it in the paper. Frank and I don't know any hustlers. They can't afford us."

Clarisse unhooked the French flag and stood, draping the smock over the chair. "Well," she said, "got to run. I'll call you next week for another appointment, Raymond."

"I'm almost done here, Clarisse."

"Listen," said Boots, "when I see Bill, I'll tell him he ought to bring you with him next time. Funny he's never mentioned you before. You want to make a date? I don't have my calendar with me, but I think next Friday night's OK."

"Oh," said Clarisse lightly, "just talk it over with Bill. I let him make all the decisions." She unsnapped her envelope, extracted several bills, and slid them into the drawer of Raymond's cabinet. "This will take care of everything."

"I'll be right back," he told Boots and laid aside his comb and scissors. He took up Clarisse's coat and walked her to the front door.

"If she starts talking about Puerto Rico," said Clarisse, "just play along."

"What is this all about?" Raymond demanded in a hissing whisper.

She touched his shoulder and looked him seriously in the eye. "One more thing, Raymond. You can't say a word about this. It's important now. Mario Scarpetti is dropping *les flics* down on Randy Harmon and Val and some other people too. They're all getting the runaround from this cop I was talking to Boots about, and we're going to stop it—so not a word."

He frowned. "Not a word, but it's going to kill me. Why don't we kidnap Scarpetti, and drag him in here? I'd like to *do his hair!*"

"You're one of the vigilantes now." She kissed him on the cheek. "I'll explain later—all the details. Or better yet, I'll send Valentine over and he can tell you all about it. Sweet dreams, Raymond, of Mario Scarpetti, dead in a ditch."

"The Marseillaise" chimed as she shoved the door open and walked into the windy street.

Chapter Sixteen

THE SNOW HAD begun in earnest while Clarisse was in Chez Marcel; it swirled more heavily still by the time that she emerged from Bonwit Teller's with two hundred dollars' worth of perfume. As she hurried through the Public Garden, it had begun to accumulate on the lawns of brown dead grass. She spotted Veronica Lake gamboling about the Civil War memorial at the crest of Boston Common's western knoll. Valentine sat slouched on a stone bench at the base of the monument, evidently in conversation with an old man who sat beside him. She waved from a distance and he rose, sliding down the snowy hill to meet her. Veronica Lake tumbled along behind him, slipping with an almost professional comicality down the slope.

The old man on the bench stood and waved to Valentine. Valentine waved cheerily back.

"Who was that?" asked Clarisse when Valentine stood beside her.

"Silber," he replied. "Breaking and entering. Three-to-five. Got out last week. I got him a job with Harry down at the South End Florist, because I knew Silber knew all about plants."

"And he wanted to thank you?" She glanced back at the old man on the crest of the hill; he was still waving.

Valentine nodded. "He gave me this." He held up a tattered pack of cards, and after making certain that Silber could not see him, tossed them into a wastepaper basket. "The thought was nice, but I wish he had brought me something more interesting. Nothing is more boring than a deck of blue Bicycles." Valentine's hands were shoved deep into the pockets of his new leather jacket and the hood of his red sweatshirt was pulled up over his head.

"You were out here the whole time?" Clarisse said.

"Raymond didn't do much for you," Valentine said, "I can't tell any difference."

"Boots had us enthralled. Once we got her started, she didn't stop."

"What did you find out?"

"Let's walk, it's too cold to stand here."

Valentine snapped the leash around the afghan's collar, and they moved slowly through the Common. By the time they had reached the corner of Tremont and Boylston streets, Clarisse had related all that she had discovered from Boots.

"I think that poor girl stays stoned all the time so that she won't have to think about the situation she's in."

"Well," said Valentine, "she apparently puts up with it one way or another."

"I think Frank has something on her, and that's why she stays."

"You think it has anything to do with Searcy?"

"No," said Clarisse carefully, "I don't think so. She was a little nervous when we were talking about Frank, talking about the way he punches her out—apparently for no reason at all—but she was all right when she talked about Searcy. Then she was just gossiping."

"But we didn't learn much really," said Valentine.

"I guess not. But at least Boots got a decent cut out of it. And you owe me twelve-fifty—I gave Raymond twenty-five because it was his lunch hour."

"Weren't there cheaper subterfuges?"

Clarisse shrugged.

"And tell me," said Valentine, "what are you going to do when Boots tells Searcy that she ran into you at the beauty parlor and that you were asking all kinds of questions about his sex life? You all but told the woman that you had moved in with the man."

"She was stoned out of her mind. She won't remember, and even if she does, Searcy doesn't know where to find me."

"Yes, but Clarisse, he knows where to find *me*! He finds out you were nosing around, he's going to come down on me, and I—"

"You know what, Valentine?"

"What?"

"You have a very negative attitude toward adventure."

Valentine threw up his hands in exasperation.

They were on the edge of the Combat Zone. Valentine looked up Boylston Street at the unlighted neon sign over Nexus. Even so early in the day there were two hustlers cowering in the doorway, staring hungrily at male passersby. No one looked back. To his left, in the opposite direction, the Combat Zone was fully lighted and busy with the remnants of the businessmen's lunch hour.

When the light changed, Valentine and Clarisse crossed and continued down Tremont toward Bay Village and the South End. "Well," said Clarisse, "as long as we're going in this direction, I might as well stop in at the office for an hour or two, see what's happening."

As they were passing the Art Cinema, Clarisse stopped under the small marquee and brushed the snow out of Veronica Lake's hair. She smiled up at Valentine. "By the way, how is Mark doing? Do you know?"

"I called home. He and the truck driver are probably going to have their blood tested; it's going to be wedding bells in the logging camp."

"Ah," said Clarisse, and straightened up, "love in the wilderness...oh!"

A male patron, departing from the cinema, had collided brusquely with Clarisse. The man glanced up at her to offer his apologies but abruptly averted his face, mumbled incoherently, and walked swiftly away from them. Startled and a bit offended by his rudeness, Clarisse righted herself. Valentine glanced back only in time to see the man's overcoat flapping against the cold wind, and his gray head drawing down against the snow. His trousers were of a shade of green rarely seen anywhere except on a Mexican postcard.

Clarisse glanced at the poster by the box office: a gaudy illustration for a film of dubious redeeming social value entitled *Hot Queers in Bondage*. It apparently had to do with the kidnapping and sexual molestation of five airline flight attendants by an equal number of men in motorcycle jackets.

"Do you think the film's as good as the poster?"

"No," said Valentine definitely.

They separated at the edge of Bay Village; Clarisse went on to the real estate office and Valentine returned to his apartment.

Chapter Seventeen

SOUTH END REALTY, sandwiched between a run-down doughnut shop and a Chinese laundry, came into view as Clarisse and Veronica Lake came round the Cyclorama Building and crossed Tremont Street against the light.

The offices were situated in the converted basement and parlor level of a four-story brick townhouse. Fine iron grillwork spread across the front of the building, with gates opening to the original stoop and to the sunken entrance of the rental office. Clarisse swung open the smaller gate and sprinted down the three salt-covered steps. She kicked open the door and swept into the office, with Veronica Lake trotting in after.

Clarisse stopped dead at the receptionist's desk. A young woman sat behind it, idly leafing through the latest issue of *Vogue* and nibbling a square of cheap chocolate. She turned a page, equally oblivious to Clarisse's presence and the ringing telephone on her desk.

Clarisse looked about. In the back of the room, Richie sat at his desk with his back to her and talked on another line. The other three desks were empty. Another voice, muffled, drifted down the staircase from the parlor level.

Clarisse stared at the receptionist, or rather, at her hair. She had never seen a style quite to match it: bangs began at the crown of the girl's head and swept forward to the top of her eyebrows, and all the rest was an ingenious construction of curls and finger waves. The woman, clearly in her early thirties, was wearing a pink jumper that she must have searched all Boston for.

"Where's Dennis?" Clarisse demanded.

The woman raised her wide heart-shaped face. "Would you like to see an agent?"

"Where's Dennis?" Clarisse repeated.

Richie swung his chair about and beamed a smile. He wound up his conversation and slipped the receiver into the cradle. "Darlene sacked him," he grinned. Darlene was the office manager.

"What?"

"Would you like an application?" The receptionist handed Clarisse a long sheet of printed paper.

"Who are you?" said Clarisse evenly. She took the application.

"Miggie Green."

Clarisse wadded the sheet of paper into a tight ball and tossed it to Richie at the back of the room. "*Miggie?*" Richie caught it.

The woman attempted a sweet smile. "Sort of a twist on Meg."

"I've no doubt," said Clarisse, her eyes wide with wonder. "Are you the new receptionist?"

Miggie Green straightened in her chair. "May I help you? Do you want to see one of our agents?"

"I *am* one of your agents," said Clarisse, with ice. She unfastened the leash and pointed Veronica Lake to the wicker sofa. The afghan trotted over and curled beneath it, resting her long sharp face on her forepaws.

The telephone on the receptionist's desk was still ringing.

"I think you have a call, Mickey," said Clarisse, and moved toward the back of the room. Miggie placed her hand on the receiver, about to lift it, but it stopped ringing. She shrugged

and picked up her chocolate bar again. Richie rolled his eyes at
Clarisse and sighed.

"Why do we have to put up with Little Miss Muff here?"
asked Clarisse loudly. "Why did Darlene fire Dennis?"

"He caught her in a kickback deal with that cute plumber,"
Richie whispered. "She tried to get rid of him before he said
anything, but you know Dennis. He ran screaming upstairs
and spilled the beans. Darlene's on the grill in the back office
right now." Richie leaned back in his chair and propped his feet
on the desk. He was very tall and slim. He yawned, brushed a
wayward blond wave back from his forehead and winked one
blue eye at Clarisse. "Miss Green is a temporary. Miss Green
has perfect sight and hearing, which supposedly qualify her to
be a receptionist/accountant. She can type a scorching thirty
words a minute, and add three small digits in her head. I
thought you were on your deathbed?"

"Oh," said Clarisse, "actually I feel a lot better now..."

Clarisse turned to drop her bag on her desk and stopped.
The entire surface of the desk had been cleared of personal
artifacts and was now piled high with neat stacks of manila
envelopes.

Clarisse turned livid. "What is this? Christ, I take a long
lunch and my desk is turned into a filing cabinet!" She bent
forward and with a wide dramatic sweep of her arm pushed all
the envelopes onto the floor in front of the desk.

Miggie Green jumped up, threw a chocolate-stained hand
over her mouth, and screeched briefly.

"Clarisse," said Richie. He dropped his feet onto the floor
heavily.

"I still work here, Richie!" Clarisse shouted. "Darlene may
not like my hours, but I pull in a lot of commissions." Clarisse
wrestled her coat off, tossed it over the back of the chair and
threw herself into it, so that it spun across the floor and banged
against the wall.

Miggie stared at her, and Clarisse shot back a glance of
loathing.

"Clarisse..." said Richie again.

"Richie," she cried, "what's happening around here?"

"Lovelace!" cried Richie. "Those envelopes are all yours. Copies of last year's leases. End of the year audit. I made Miggie dig them all out so that you wouldn't have to."

Clarisse lowered her brows by degrees. She sighed and went around the desk to retrieve the envelopes. Richie stood to help her.

"How's Daniel?" asked Richie, when they had restacked them.

"He's trying to convince me to go with him to St. Kitts." Clarisse opened the middle drawer of her desk and extracted her listings and appointment books. Fumbling in the back she pulled out a pack of Kools and an ashtray. She lit a cigarette and sat back, crossing her legs. "I can't decide whether I really want to go or not, though."

A door slammed loudly above, and heavy feet crossed to the stairs. In one motion, Richie and Clarisse turned face front. "Here comes the *Hindenburg*," Richie mumbled.

A great shadow fell across the office as the body of an immensely fat woman blocked the light from the chandelier in the ceiling of the office above. Darlene was six feet tall, which she imagined excused her for weighing close to three hundred pounds.

An orange pantsuit was tortured around her body. It had several times split up the back and was sewn there with purple thread, thick as yarn. Her waist-length black cape flapped about her as she strode across the office toward the door. She ran her hands violently through her short dyed yellow hair, and stared wildly about. "I'm mad," she hissed between clenched teeth. "I'm so mad I could bite the sink!"

She pulled the door open so that it hit the inside wall with a shuddering crash. She sidled through the doorway, and lumbered up the steps. On the sidewalk she plowed through a group of Chinese schoolchildren and tumbled three little girls into a snowbank.

Clarisse and Richie exchanged glances. "I guess the heat was on high," he said.

Richie picked up the phone and turned his back again. Clarisse checked through her listing book. After a few moments a short young man entered the office, ignored Miggie Green, and went straight back to Clarisse. He handed her a sealed white envelope.

"Rent," he gasped. "I was hoping you'd be here."

"Hi, Lewis," she smiled. She dropped the envelope into a drawer.

"I thought you had hepatitis or something."

"It was malaria," she said, "but I'm cured."

"My radiator's leaking," he whispered. "And the toilet's running and I can't get it to stop. Something's wrong with the hinges on the bedroom door." He paused. "I think the whole door needs replacing."

Clarisse sighed. "What did you and George fight about this time?"

Lewis threw himself into a chair, and rested his elbows on Clarisse's desk. "He's gone, Clarisse, he left for good this time."

"Lewis, the first time George left for good, we had to put in a new bathtub—and George came back. The second time George left for good, we had to replaster all your walls—and George came back. This time we'll put in a new radiator—and George will come back."

Lewis rubbed his sunken, haggard eyes. Clarisse offered him a cigarette, and had to light it for him when his hands trembled on his matches.

"He won't come back," he murmured. "He wouldn't come back even if you put in a skylight. He's gone back to his ex-lover."

"How much money do you have in the bank?" asked Clarisse.

"Don't worry. I can still pay the rent."

"I didn't mean that."

He shrugged. "About a thousand. Why?"

"Draw it out—today. Tomorrow at the latest, and book the first flight to San Francisco. Believe me, after a week of debauchery in the shadow of the Golden Gate you won't even remember who George was."

"George is *in* San Francisco. That's where his ex is."

Clarisse frowned and thought a moment. "Aruba. Go to Aruba, Lewis."

"Nobody goes to Aruba for a week."

"But *you* will. It's great this time of year. Val and I were just there. Don't even stop to think about it." She grabbed a scrap of paper, and jotted down a name and number. "This is my friend Marcia at Continental Tours. Tell her you're a friend of mine and she'll give you a terrific discount." Lewis nodded, took the paper and left.

Clarisse ground her cigarette in the ashtray and stared out the front window. The snow continued. She had realized, while she was talking to Lewis, that there was something that she ought to tell Valentine: something that he ought to know, or perhaps that she ought to know herself. But she couldn't think what it was. She picked up her listing book again. If it was important, it would come to her later.

Chapter Eighteen

"**J**OSEPH'S GOING TO drive me back with him, Daniel," said Mark.

When Valentine had returned to his apartment after leaving Clarisse, he found Mark sitting in the living room, his pack on the floor at his feet. He looked as if he were waiting for a train.

"Where is he?" Valentine asked, as he removed his new jacket and placed it carefully on a chair. He patted it and smiled at Mark.

"Putting gas in the pickup. You don't mind, do you, Daniel, my popping in and out like this, I mean?"

Valentine smiled. "You really like him, don't you?"

Mark nodded.

"And you're going to continue the whirlwind romance in New Hampshire, in the cab of the oil truck?"

Mark nodded again.

"I'm jealous."

Mark's timid smile fled. "I don't want you to be jealous."

"Not jealous of him. Jealous of you. You know how partial I am to Italian truck drivers. I'm greener than green."

Valentine made coffee and the two men talked until Joseph arrived. He did not ask them to stay longer, for he saw how anxious they were to get off together. He did, however, tell them that they had an open invitation to visit Fayette Street anytime they chose.

Standing at the bay window Valentine waved to the two men as they climbed into the pickup, and then watched as it disappeared around a corner. He hadn't even had time to turn around, before a green '56 Chrysler New Yorker pulled up into the same spot. When Randy Harmon stepped out, Valentine raised the window and leaned out. Randy held one hand over his eyes to shield them against the falling snow.

"Come on up," called Valentine. "I've just been abandoned, without being seduced."

"I'm having an anxiety attack, Valentine."

Valentine sighed. "Dr. Usen's not in town?"

Randy dropped his hand at his side. "Venezuela. World Hypnotism Conference. I'm in a bad way, Valentine. You'll have to go to the Green Grocer with me."

Valentine nodded and pulled back inside. After lowering the window he slipped on his jacket, took extra money from the desk, and ran downstairs.

Randy was sitting on the passenger side of the front seat. Valentine was fond of the car and Randy always let him drive whenever they went anywhere together. Valentine climbed in, and sighed contentedly as he released the brake and depressed one of the panel buttons to put the car in gear. As they pulled away from the curb, Valentine ritualistically pressed more buttons—to push the front seat forward and back and then up and down. The last button turned on the radio.

"So," he said at last, "why the anxiety?"

"Actually, I lied to you. I feel fine—I really did have an attack, but Dr. Usen left me cassette tapes when he went away, so I just played through the one marked 'Anxiety,' and it was just like having him there. But I still thought I needed to get out of the city for a while, and I do have to go to the Green Grocer. I've got a crave on for endive."

"You tricked me," said Valentine. He gripped the large steering wheel hard. "You know how I hate the suburbs. It's a jungle out there, Randy."

"You'll get over it. Besides, you can buy veg too."

Valentine drove through the city and got onto Route 93 heading north toward New Hampshire. The Green Grocer was a specialty store about ten miles out of town; it carried a certain kind of pear from Morocco, and fresh lichees from China, and little potatoes from a tiny farm on the Snake River, and half a dozen kinds of fungi from Japan. They had discovered the place when they shared an apartment in Medford while students at Tufts, and now returned as much for the nostalgia as for the fine vegetables.

Shopping there took three-quarters of an hour, since everything was worth examining even when they had no intention of purchasing Brazilian melons that went for six dollars apiece, and Randy took over for the drive back to Boston. He got back onto Route 93, but went only two exits before turning off again.

"Where are you going?" cried Valentine. "This isn't Boston yet!"

The light was beginning to fail as a blue winter dusk gathered about them.

"I want to show you something—"

"What!"

"Valentine, don't get panicky. We haven't been out of the city much more than an hour. You're not going to have a breakdown yet."

Valentine slid down in his seat as the car moved through streets lined with large houses set back on neat, snow-covered lawns. "How much further?" he groaned.

"We've only gone six blocks, Valentine."

"I'm not going to have to meet anybody, am I? If I meet somebody and he invites me to a party or something, expecting that I'll come back out here again, I'm going to kill you."

"You don't have to meet anybody." Randy swung the car around a corner and up a slight grade. Valentine could see that the street ended in a cul-de-sac.

"You're taking me to meet somebody, I know it!"

"No, I'm not," said Randy, and stopped the car. He got out and motioned Valentine to follow.

Valentine sighed and climbed out. He moved around to the front of the car. He smiled broadly, lifted his arms and pivoted from the waist. "Oh, God, it's beautiful out here! It's just beautiful! So much nicer than the city! The air is clean, the light is gorgeous, the snow is clean and untrampled!" He shook the falling snow from his outstretched arms—"Now let's get the hell back to Boston."

Randy pointed at a row of hemlocks just on the other side of a concrete walk. "The scene of the crime," he said quietly.

Valentine looked down. The ground was slightly more uneven here than it was on the lawn behind the evergreens, but otherwise he saw nothing to distinguish the place. He glanced up at the large stucco house beyond the linden and spruce.

"That's Scarpetti's house?"

Randy nodded.

"Why did you bring me here?" said Valentine.

Randy shrugged. "Why not? If Searcy's going to try to pin this thing on me, I want to know exactly where it was that I dumped the kid. Actually," he said, looking about, "I wouldn't mind living around here. It sure beats the hell out of Goodwin Place."

They turned to get back in the car but halted immediately. Randy drew in a sharp breath.

Standing motionless at the back of the Chrysler was a tall bearded man in a fur coat. The red pulsating light of the car's directional signal was reflected off his round-lensed eyeglasses.

"Your treads are too wide," he said.

Valentine and Randy exchanged puzzled glances.

"To be the 'death car,' I mean. Of course, you could have had your tires changed to avoid detection, or you might have been driving a somewhat less recognizable automobile."

Professor Philip Lawrence stepped forward. He lifted his glasses, and looked carefully from Randy to Valentine. He dropped his glasses back in place.

"Valentine and...ummm, Harmony," he announced.

"Harmon," said Randy. "Professor Lawrence?"

Lawrence smiled. "I never forget history majors, especially when they're...blond."

"Sorry," said Valentine, "I didn't recognize you at first, in the dusk."

"No excuse. It's been only nine years."

Lawrence invited them inside the house to get warm. Once they were settled comfortably in the living room before a blazing birch fire, Neville served them sherry and a kind of Chinese tea roll neither Valentine nor Randy had ever had before. Their conversation centered naturally around the murder of the hustler, and Randy and Valentine each told his connection with it.

"Of course, there's no doubt that Scarpetti's upset," said Lawrence with a gentle smile, "because he's had a dozen cars in front of his house every night, cronies to talk over the matter and whatnot. Police cruise up and down the street every ten minutes, all night long, guarding against a repetition of the embarrassment. He's had floodlights installed on the side of the house, and they shine directly in my windows. I'm furious about that. When all this dies down, I have a friend who's promised to come down from New Hampshire and shoot them out for me. I can imagine that Scarpetti's coming down hard on the Boston cops—O'Brien's a good friend of his. They've even put a watch on me, I think, because Scarpetti told them that he lives directly across the street from a known, practicing, avowed homosexual—though I don't think he has the sense to have figured out exactly what my relationship to Neville is—but surveillance I don't mind particularly, as long as they don't ring my doorbell..."

When Lawrence then discovered that he had in fact been visited by the same Boston policeman who loomed so large in the consciousnesses of Randy and Valentine, he said, "The thing that struck me odd about him, other than the fact that he said he was straight, was that it seemed that all he wanted was to be sure that I *hadn't* seen the body being disposed of. He didn't much care for my thoughts on the matter, which were a great deal more developed than his own. He seemed, in fact, almost relieved that I hadn't seen anything the night before."

"I don't think he likes this assignment," said Valentine.

"No," said Lawrence, "and I can't really blame him. As murders go, it's not very sensational. That little boy wasn't much more interesting in death than he was in life. That's one reason I found it odd that Searcy would come around to talk to me when he was off duty. I even had the impression, I'm not sure now why, that he was doing a little of this on his own."

Randy laughed. "He seems to do a lot of his work on this case when he's off duty."

Valentine laid his hand across his heart, cocked his head, and said, "Ah to be sure, William Searcy is a dedicated cop. True blue to his very wee soul."

"Daniel," said Lawrence, "your Irish accent is abominable. You should never use it in public. But there's something strange there. Policemen, probably more than members of other professions, value their off-duty hours..."

Lawrence paused while Neville passed around another plate of the strange biscuits.

"Well," said Randy, "maybe off duty's the time when he works best."

"No," said Lawrence, "he didn't seem a very efficient worker. A good investigator always does his homework, and Searcy hadn't done any of his. The best thing about him was his name. And of course he was rather good looking, in a Marine Corps poster sort of way..."

"Well," said Valentine, draining the last of his sherry, "it may be that Lieutenant Searcy has a few surprises for us by the time that all of this is done with."

Chapter Nineteen

VALENTINE HADN'T closed the door behind him when the telephone began ringing. It rang ten times while he put his bag of vegetables on the kitchen table, carefully hung up his jacket, and removed his boots.

"Yes?" he said placidly as he picked up the receiver.

"*Where* have you been?" Clarisse shrieked. "I've been calling you every ten minutes since five-thirty!"

"Clarisse," he said, "it's only six. I went with Randy up to the Green Grocer, and then we ran into an old professor of ours—"

She cut him off. "Val," she cried breathlessly, "I had a revelation!" Traffic ground loudly behind her voice.

Valentine rose from the couch and carried the telephone into the kitchen.

"Where are you?" he said.

"In a phone booth, with Veronica Lake." He heard the dog's bark, and its echo. "I couldn't wait until I got home. Remember that man who bumped into me by the Art Cinema?"

"Yes."

"Remember what he looked like?"

Valentine stared out the window at the increasing snow. "An overcoat that didn't fit particularly well, and a pair of green slacks that somebody should have put a torch to."

"No, his face!"

"I didn't see it. What is this, Clarisse?" He leaned against the windowsill.

"I did see his face, in profile, but only for a second."

"Yes..." said Val encouragingly, when she paused.

"It was Trudy...!" she whispered.

Valentine said nothing for a moment. He heard Veronica Lake bark again, this time more loudly.

"Go away! Shoo!" cried Clarisse. "There's another afghan outside the booth, trying to get in! Shoo!"

"What do you mean 'Trudy'? Clarisse, that man had pants on. Trudy doesn't wear pants. I'd be surprised if she even *owned* a pair of pants. Trudy wouldn't be seen in public dressed like a man."

"It was Trudy, Val!" Clarisse drew in her breath sharply. "Listen, you've never seen Trudy out of drag, have you?"

"No I haven't, and I don't know anybody who has."

"Now you do. She bumped into me, and turned profile. How can you forget Trudy's profile? The only reason I didn't recognize her at first was because she wasn't wearing any makeup, and she didn't have on any kind of wig. And I've never seen Trudy without makeup and a wig, so it didn't register at first."

Valentine laughed. "No wonder she was anxious to run away from us." He took a breath and fished a cigarette from the pack in his back pocket. He lit it and dropped the match into an ashtray. "And you've locked yourself in a telephone booth with Veronica Lake so that you could call me up and tell me this?"

"Of course not," said Clarisse with some exasperation. "This is important. Remember the description that Mack and Randy gave of the man that had picked up Billy at Nexus?"

"Yes," said Valentine hesitantly.

"Well," said Clarisse, "it fits."

"Fits? Fits what?"

"Fits Trudy. They gave a description of what Trudy looks like when she's out of drag. It was Trudy in civilian clothes that picked up little Billy Golacinsky."

"Clarisse, you're out of your mind. Just because Trudy puts on ugly green pants and a trench coat and goes to the porn flicks, doesn't mean that she also goes out and bludgeons little boys to death."

"No, of course not," said Clarisse, "but there was something else—" Suddenly Veronica Lake set up a ferocious barking, and it took a little while for Clarisse to calm her down. "Veronica Lake," she cried, "has just ripped my best seamed stockings!"

"What else?" demanded Valentine, glad that he was not stuck in a telephone booth with a large dog when it was snowing out.

"Remember when we were in Nexus and I asked Searcy what color lipstick was on Billy's handkerchief?"

"Yes—you certainly did go on about that too."

"He said it was a darker shade than the color I was wearing, and that would make it vermilion, Val. Vermilion! Trudy wore vermilion lipstick, it was the only color that she ever wore, but she told me that she gave it up on New Year's Day. That little boy was killed on New Year's Day!"

"And that's your evidence to prove that Trudy killed William A. Golacinsky?"

"Yes."

"Trudy has never struck me as the homicidal type."

"Lizzie Borden didn't look like a killer either."

"But Richard Speck did." He paused, then said, "I think maybe you're right. I'm certainly not going to call up Searcy, but I think we ought to have a little talk with Trudy."

"I ought to be there too."

"Of course. Can you be at the bar by ten?"

Chapter Twenty

VALENTINE WAS preoccupied all that evening, unable to take his mind from the possibility that Trudy, with whom he had maintained an affectionate relationship since the time he had come to work at Bonaparte's, had brutally murdered a nineteen-year-old boy. He was relieved when the bar began to fill and he was kept busy, but he was momentarily distracted when Trudy entered shortly after ten. He wondered if it were only his projection, or whether her greeting to him seemed curt and embarrassed.

Trudy played Rodgers and Hammerstein, but in a muddy spiritless fashion. The drink that Valentine had sent over to her sat untouched on top of the piano.

It wasn't until half past ten that Valentine saw Clarisse handing her coat over to Irene in the checkroom. She had changed into black cord slacks and a white-and-red reindeer sweater.

Valentine motioned the waiter over, and told him that he would have to manage the bar for a while. "You'll only be on for half an hour, and I'll double whatever tips you make—OK?" The waiter nervously agreed.

As Valentine approached, Clarisse was removing her gloves and stuffing them into her leather envelope. Valentine took her right hand and examined the two adhesive bandages around her index finger and thumb.

"What happened this time?"

"Oh, Val, after I talked to you I got so upset thinking about Trudy that I cut myself slicing a plum tomato." She thrust her hand into her pocket. "You don't look so cheery yourself."

"Oh, it's been a great evening! Scarpetti's paranoia is making the rounds. Cops raided the South Station Cinema this afternoon, and arrested my friend Jim who was running the projector. And Cal dropped in here a couple of hours ago to tell me that *Today's Boston* is running an article next month called, 'Bonaparte's Blown Apart: Haven for High-Priced Hustlers.' Mostly I'm worried about this thing with Trudy, though." He smiled weakly. "Let's get it over with."

Clarisse glanced at the clock behind the bar. "About time for her break, isn't it?"

"Yes."

Clarisse took a deep breath. "You stay here and let me speak to her for a minute."

Clarisse moved past him and made her way to the Wicker Room.

Trudy was playing a halfhearted clumsy flourish to conclude "You'll Never Walk Alone." When she saw Clarisse sidling through a knot of men, she snatched up her drink and downed it.

She turned to Clarisse and smiled. "Good evening dear."

"Is this your break?" Clarisse seated herself beside Trudy on the piano bench.

Trudy nodded.

"I'd like to talk to you about something personal, if you could spare me a few minutes," said Clarisse.

"Personal to who? You or me?"

"Me."

Trudy took a swallow from the drink that was nothing but ice. "Is it a 'woman's problem'?"

Clarisse nodded, and engineered a soft smile.

"Well, dear, we can't very well discuss such things around a piano, with all these good-looking men about." Trudy nudged Clarisse, and then slid off the bench.

"Step into my office," said Trudy, and led Clarisse toward the restrooms. She stuck her head inside the ladies' room door and cried, "This is Trudy! I'm serving eviction notices!"

While Trudy's back was turned, Clarisse raised her arm and waved it as a signal for Valentine to follow. He had been hovering near the door of the Wicker Room and now stepped forward.

A middle-aged man in a three-piece suit emerged from the ladies' room, said with a tender smile, "It's all yours," and moved away to rejoin his friends.

Clarisse and Trudy stepped inside. Clarisse leaned against the mirror, and Trudy stepped into the last stall. She put down the seat cover and sat comfortably, crossing her legs so that one green wedgie propped open the door of the stall.

"Let me guess," said Trudy, "you finally cornered Valentine and now you're pregnant."

"No," said Clarisse, "that's not it exactly."

The door opened.

"Full house!" warbled Trudy in falsetto.

Valentine stepped in without a word, closed the door carefully behind him and crossed to lean against the sink.

Trudy glanced from one to the other. "All right," she said, in a low somber voice, "what's up?"

"Trudy," said Clarisse, "I saw you this afternoon—"

"Yes," said Trudy quickly. "Coming out of the Art Cinema. I thought that you hadn't recognized me—but it was me, all right. And you two are upset? I thought you of all people would be a little more understanding. I may dress like a woman of fashion, but there are times that I still like to go into a dark theater and watch little boys do nasty things on the silver screen, and I couldn't get into the place looking like this."

"Of course we're not upset about that," said Clarisse, "we—"

"We want to know what you know about Billy Golacinsky," said Valentine, more harshly than he'd intended.

Trudy uncrossed her legs, and the door of the stall swung shut. In a moment she pushed it open again, crossed her legs the other way, and now braced the door with her knee. She righted her wig. "Who?"

"You know who we're talking about," said Clarisse softly.

"What was his name? Willy?"

Valentine took a cigarette from his jeans and lit it. "We're not accusing you, Trudy. We just want to know what you know."

She suddenly left off her fidgeting. "Billy Golacinsky was a hustler. He got murdered. He got his picture in the paper and he got a berth in the city morgue. What else do you want to know?"

Valentine and Clarisse said nothing. Their boots scraped loudly against the white-tiled floor. Trudy fished a pack of cigarettes from the bodice of her green print dress. Valentine leaned forward to light it for her. She propped one arm up on the paper dispenser and looked at them steadily. "I met him Monday night..."

"At Nexus," said Valentine.

She nodded. "I had worked all New Year's Eve here, of course, and that little boy was going to be my way of ringing in the new year. You know," she said, more softly, "most people that look at me think all my sexuality goes into my drag, but that's not quite true. I'm usually up for a little give-and-take, but after a certain age—well, you have to pay for it."

Clarisse smiled weakly. "Of course, there's nothing wrong with that either, Trudy."

Trudy nodded briefly. "So anyway, I was at Nexus Monday night. Not in drag. Actually, I don't have much character when I'm out of drag, I'm just an anonymous old man." She glanced at Clarisse. "By the way, how did you know it was me this afternoon?"

"Your profile."

Trudy touched her nose ruefully, but said nothing. "I saw this little boy sitting at the bar, and he had everything but a sign around his neck that said 'Twenty-five Dollars.' In my mind, I called him 'Dondi'—the cold, wet, hungry orphan. So I sent over drinks to try to get him drunk. We left there about..."

"One-thirty," said Valentine.

She nodded. "Of course, I wasn't going to take him home. He looked the kind who might have fingers for plastic. And I might need my American Express next time I fly to San Juan. I didn't trust him."

"Then why did you bother?" asked Valentine.

"A girl can't sit at home knitting *every* night. I knew he didn't have a place either, and if he did, I certainly wasn't going there, so I suggested the baths."

The door of the restroom opened and a large burly man with a bushy black beard and wearing a black leather jacket stepped inside. "Oh sorry," he said, "family council. I'll come back later—I just wanted to take out my contacts." He left.

"You suggested the baths?" asked Valentine. "Randy Harmon told me Billy usually suggested that."

"I've been to the baths before but Randy's never recognized me, and of course I pretend that I don't know him. I turned my face away, just in case. But I wondered why that little boy got so excited when I mentioned the Royal. And then when we were going up in the elevator, he said I had to call him 'Duke Wayne.' Can you imagine? I thought, 'Well honey, you got yourself a fruitcake this time!' We stayed awhile, and then I drove him back to Park Square and that was the last I saw of him until you showed me that morgue shot, Clarisse. I would have said something then but I wanted to make sure I wasn't going to be fingered. A woman of my stature ought not be fingered. Now," she said, gathering her skirts about her, "can I go back and earn my beads?"

"No," said Clarisse.

"You don't believe me?"

Valentine shrugged. "You left things out. We want to know what happened at the baths. You and Billy didn't stay long enough to have a real session, and he was angry when you two left."

Trudy shrugged and sighed. "All right, listen. Of course when we went in, I had my bag…"

"The doctor's bag?" asked Clarisse.

"Actually it's just an overnight bag I picked up last time Rochelle and I went to Germany. So we got in the room, and the kid was taking off his clothes and I opened the bag and took out my makeup and my wig. I was putting on the new earrings I had gotten for Christmas…"

"And he got upset?" said Valentine.

Trudy nodded, embarrassed. "You'd think he'd never seen a man get dressed up before. He started to call me names, said he wasn't going to go through with it, that it was bad enough to have to do it with an old man, much less with an old woman—and so on. He demanded twice the amount we had agreed on, and of course I said no, especially since he wasn't going through with anything. Then he said that the least I could do was drive him back to Park Square so that he could make some more money. I told him he'd probably be better off if he just stayed at the baths where he was warm and dry, but he was still loaded and said he had to make more money. Very nasty little boy—no manners at all. So I dropped him off in Park Square—and I can verify that."

"How?" said Clarisse.

"Because when he got out of the car, I saw my friend Jolanda Watson standing up against the wall, and she saw Billy get out. Jolanda sometimes works the Square."

Clarisse folded her arms, and leaned back against the mirror again. "When did you kiss Billy? In the room at the baths?"

Trudy drew back in surprise. "I didn't kiss him! I didn't want to. Bad skin. Once he started calling me names, I got turned off. I didn't even touch him."

"Then how did the vermilion lipstick get on his handker-chief? That's how we knew you had been with him."

Trudy shrugged. "I don't know. I didn't put it there. I told you I swore off the stuff on New Year's Eve. I wasn't wearing my lipstick that night."

"Come on, Trudy," said Clarisse. "You had lipstick on last Tuesday, but then the murder was in the papers and you didn't put it on again."

"That was the night I got so upset. I couldn't get the car started, and then I broke my heel. When I went back to the house to change my shoes I had to have something to cheer me up, so I took out the tube that I had been saving for the undertaker and put that on—that made me feel better. But the next day I realized what I had done, so I put the tube in my safety deposit box at the bank because I didn't want to be tempted again."

Clarisse and Valentine nodded; they believed her.

"So," said Valentine, "you left Billy in Park Square and that was the last you saw of him."

Trudy pulled off a long streamer of toilet tissue and blew her nose. "No," she said, "it wasn't."

"You saw him again!" cried Clarisse.

"Well," said Trudy, "when I let him out, Jolanda got in and made me drive her around until she got warm again. So I just kept going around the block, and the first time I went around he was there, leaning up against the bus station, but the second time I went around he was climbing into a car that had two men in it, one in the front seat and one in the back."

She wadded the toilet tissue in her hand and stood, lifted the lid and dropped it inside. She flushed the toilet and stepped out of the stall. Clarisse backed out of her way and Valentine dropped down off the sink to allow her to get to the mirror.

Now Clarisse and Valentine flanked her, and they stared hard while she checked her makeup.

"What kind of a car?" said Clarisse.

"An old beat-up thing. I was thinking that whoever drove a car like that couldn't afford to pay much, but that maybe the two men were going to split the fee. Except probably it turned out that they were fag-baiters, and they beat him up and killed him…"

"Billy wasn't beat up," said Valentine, "he was hit only once, and that killed him…"

"Do you remember anything else about the car?"

"It was old and beat up, no class. I mean, it was blue and then it had a green front fender."

Valentine's mouth dropped open. "Green front fender?"

Trudy nodded and pinched her cheeks to put color into them. "I hope you two have not been going around all day thinking it was me that killed that little boy. How could a woman with a repertoire of seven hundred show tunes be guilty of murder?"

Clarisse leaned forward and kissed her on the cheek. "This thing has been on our minds," she said apologetically. "That cop has been getting on our nerves."

Trudy smiled and patted Clarisse's hand.

Valentine smiled as Trudy moved past him and went back out into the Wicker Room. He turned to face Clarisse across the sink. "Frank Hougan," he said. "Billy Golacinsky got into Frank Hougan's car the night he was murdered."

Chapter Twenty-one

BY TWO-THIRTY Saturday morning, Bonaparte's was quiet. Irene and Trudy had accompanied the last two customers out. As soon as Jack had finished sweeping up on the second floor, he left with the black-bearded man who had wanted to remove his contacts in the ladies' restroom.

Valentine was alone. He fixed himself a strong drink, his first of the night, and sat at the bar with it. A few cars drove past outside, their tires loudly crunching the layer of fresh snow that had fallen earlier. Valentine smoked two cigarettes and forced himself to think not of Billy Golacinsky or Trudy or Boots or Hougan or Searcy or even of Clarisse but rather of the two offers to go home that he had turned down earlier. His refusals had been polite but automatic, and he wondered now why he had been so hasty.

After rinsing his glass, he threw his jacket over his arm and checked the entire place to make sure that the lights were out. He left only the bulb in the foyer on, and after securing the heavy iron front door and setting the alarm system, he turned his steps homeward.

The temperature had dropped considerably, but there was mercifully no wind. Valentine zipped his jacket to the throat and made fists in his pockets as he rounded the corner onto Cedar Street. He was relieved to be out of sight of the Howard Johnson's Motor Lodge, which looked like a concrete-and-neon mausoleum.

Just before he reached a small brick townhouse where he had once accompanied someone home, a fist slammed squarely into his back, and Valentine's breath forsook him in one groaning blast. His feet slipped on the snow as he reeled forward, and his arms flew up. He fell sideways onto the concrete, and his head *thunk*ed solidly against the curbing. He doubled up from intense pain and the instinctive fear of being kicked in the head.

Strong bare hands seized his shoulders and he was dragged across the sidewalk. Cinders and ice tore open the side of his face.

Valentine struggled to turn himself over, but the toe of a man's boot bashed hard into the small of his back. He groaned again and his legs shot out. The strong hands slipped under his arms. The dark silent street flashed by as he was roughly lifted and then slammed down again on his stomach. His knees hit a sharp stone and he realized that he was being shoved into a darkened recess between two brick buildings.

He struggled to get to one side, but a knee was jammed between his shoulder blades, and then a tiny circle of cold steel was pressed against his neck. Hot breath and the nauseating smell of half-digested bourbon welled up against Valentine's cheek.

"Listen you bastard..." a slurred guttural voice hissed in his ear.

A car rounded the corner a few dozen yards down and headlights fanned across the buildings just above them. Valentine was suddenly released.

The same voice, already retreating, growled, "Don't turn around..." Then Valentine heard heavy footsteps through the snow.

The car turned again at the next corner. Bay Village was quiet again.

Valentine slowly and painfully laid himself prone, more for the comfort of the snow against the burning cuts on his face than for any protection he thought the position afforded. He feared that his attacker lay in wait in another doorway, his gun cocked and aimed.

Valentine crawled around the stoop of the house nearest him, in the direction opposite from the way his assailant had fled. Once on the other side, he sat up and pushed himself into the corner, his back pressing against a newly planted holly shrub.

The clear clanging of a church bell signaled the hour. Valentine realized abruptly that he was in considerable pain, his stomach and his back aching very badly. He pulled his knees up and rested his head between them. He sat still a minute more, then vomited. Afterward, he leaned against the stoop with closed eyes, taking in long deep breaths, and stayed until the cold air had cleared his head.

Valentine struggled to his feet and, staying close to the brick walls and always in the darkest shadows, made his way down Fayette Street.

Once inside his apartment he bolted the door, slipped off his jacket and collapsed on his back on the sofa. He groaned miserably with volume that he hadn't allowed himself in the open air. Without turning on any lights he pulled the phone across the floor by its cord and dialed quickly. It rang six times before Clarisse answered. "This better be good," she said in a garbled thick voice.

"It's great," said Valentine.

"What's wrong?" She recognized his voice, and the tone of it alarmed her.

"Listen," he said, his breath heaving suddenly, "is your place locked? Make sure it's locked—"

"What is it, Val?" she demanded, with more urgency. "Are you hurt?"

"Make sure everything's locked, and put Veronica Lake in the living room."

"What happened?"

"Searcy's on the prowl. We ran into each other on Fayette Street."

"What happened?" she repeated, with apparent misgiving.

"He put a fist in my ribs, and a knee in my back, and a gun up against the side of my head. He was overly dramatic."

"Val, I'm coming right over. Hang up so I can call a taxi."

"Stay there! That's why I called. He's prowling around and he's out of his mind."

"Are you bleeding or anything? Did you call the doctor? Call Richard—Richard would give anything to come over and see you in the middle of the night."

"The way I look now, Clarisse, I think even Richard would be turned off. No, I'm not going to call a doctor." He touched his cheek and the thick lines of crusting blood there. The palms of his hands were raw, but the skin had broken in only a few places.

"Well, if you're not going to call the doctor, then call the police."

"No, I can't. I didn't see him, I only heard his voice. I also smelled him, same cheap bourbon. Just put Veronica Lake in the living room and don't take anything that'll make you sleep soundly. I'll be all right and I'll be over in the morning. But tonight, whatever you do, don't leave the building. Don't come over, because tonight I'm not letting *anybody* in."

"OK," said Clarisse, after a moment's hesitation.

"Got to go and lick my wounds clean. Good-night."

Clarisse eased the receiver back into the cradle and set the phone back on the floor by the bed. She threw back the covers and reached for her robe, which was keeping warm on a chair next to the radiator. She roused Veronica Lake by pushing the dog off her bed.

"Come on, girl. Tonight you're earning your keep."

Veronica Lake, expecting to go out, followed Clarisse into the dark living room. Pale light from the nearest streetlamp made two small squares of light across the floor. The window nearest the kitchen was cracked a couple of inches.

Veronica Lake became very excited as Clarisse checked the locks on the door.

"No," commanded Clarisse sternly, and much disappointed, Veronica Lake collapsed in front of the cold fireplace and immediately fell asleep.

Clarisse cautiously approached the window, and standing to one side in the shadows, she scanned the street. A single car was stopped at a light a couple of blocks down on Beacon. Nothing moved along the length of the block or around the lighted stoop beneath her window.

She was tempted to call Valentine again, but decided not to. Her eyes had accustomed to the darkness of the room; she crossed to the kitchen, filled the teakettle with water, and placed it over a high gas flame. She dumped several spoonfuls of cocoa into a mug.

She waited in the darkest corner of the kitchen, far away from the windows. She started when the branch of a dying elm scraped across one of the windows, but then she relaxed the more for its having been a false alarm.

She drank her cocoa in silence, sitting cross-legged on the floor, stroking Veronica Lake.

The scraping came again, fainter this time; but when Clarisse glanced at the window, she saw that it was not the elm. Once more, still more distinctly. She stood and moved quietly to the window.

Nothing moved in the street, but the sound continued. Abruptly the light from the entranceway winked out—someone had been unscrewing the bulb there. He was hidden by the small projecting roof of the building's stoop.

Clarisse stared downward and gasped when she saw a flash of dark sleeve and white hand from beneath the stone awning.

She drew back more. She heard a doorknob turned and turned again, and then a careful thud as weight was pressed against the door downstairs.

Clarisse rushed into the kitchen. The water in the kettle was still steaming. She shakily poured the water into a large saucepan, splashing some of it over the length of the counter.

She carried the pan of water to the living room window and rested it on the sill. Then she pushed the window up forcefully, with as loud a scrape as was possible.

Veronica Lake snapped her head up and growled. Clarisse held her breath and waited. A man backed out from underneath the entranceway and onto the front steps.

Clarisse seized the pan and dumped all the water out the window, directly toward the pale, unrecognizable face that gazed up at her.

A hand flashed up defensively, and the face was withdrawn. The scalding water splashed on the hand, and there was a short animal-like scream.

Veronica Lake snarled and barked. Clarisse dropped the pan on the floor. She thrust herself halfway out the window, gripping the sill tightly. Footsteps scraped down the stoop and a man fled up Beacon Street. He was quickly lost in the shadows.

Her eyes were wide and bright and she did not feel the bitter wind through her thick black hair and down the front of her open robe. Veronica Lake sat with her chin on the windowsill and barked; the sound echoed across the wide dark street.

Saturday, 6 January

Chapter Twenty-two

"**M**Y SOCIAL LIFE is wrecked for the next two weeks," moaned Valentine, his first lament upon reaching Clarisse's apartment on Saturday morning.

"Your social life's fine," said Clarisse, "but your sex life may suffer, unless you can find someone who's into physical disfigurement." She brought him a mug of coffee from the kitchen. Valentine didn't try to sit up, but held it against his chest.

"How do you feel?" she asked, sitting at the other end of the couch and lifting his feet to rest them in her lap. She still wore her robe.

"Like I spent the night in the trunk of somebody's Volkswagen." He stretched a muscle in his side to see if it was painful; it was. "I wonder if you burned Searcy badly enough for him to see a doctor."

"I wish it had been boiling oil. You can't imagine how virtuous I felt, trying to scald a man to death." She rested her head back against the sofa. "Val, why don't we quit fooling around and just wend our merry way over to police headquarters and tell them everything we know?"

"Cops don't like to hear nasty things about other cops. And we don't really have any proof. I didn't see the man who hit me last night, and you don't have anything but a moral certainty that it was Searcy that was trying to break into this building. All we know for sure is that he plays not very interesting little games with Mr. and Ms. Leatherette. Speaking of whom, I talked to Jack last night and he remembered seeing Hougan in Bonaparte's before. He goes upstairs and meets a doctor from Peter Bent Brigham Hospital that Jack knows."

"So—Searcy's word against ours."

Valentine nodded.

"I have an alternative plan," said Clarisse.

"What?"

"We'll both get dressed up, and pretend we're taking a leisurely stroll over toward District One station, but just before we get there, we'll run across the street to the Eastern Airlines office and buy two tickets to the Canary Islands. And then we'll go. To the Canary Islands. You like it?"

Valentine took a sip of his coffee. "I'd love to, but we can't run away from this. Did you see what Scarpetti said in *today's* paper?"

"Oh God! What?"

"He said that if something isn't done soon to repress the gay community, 'our children will be caught in the cross fire of a Homosexual Tong War.'"

"The man has a way with words."

"He also said that a known homosexual had confessed to the murder."

"Oh!" shrieked Clarisse. "Anybody we know?"

"He made it up," said Valentine. "Nobody confessed."

"Oh."

Valentine looked closely at Clarisse. "I want you to call someone."

"Who?"

"After I finish the coffee."

❋ ❋ ❋

An hour later Clarisse opened her apartment door to admit Boots Slater. Valentine stood, a little crookedly, at the bookshelves beside the fireplace. He was turning the radio to an FM station. He turned and nodded to Boots. Clarisse closed the door carefully behind her, then introduced Boots and Valentine.

"Oh yeah, I've seen you around. You followed me home one day, but then you didn't come through. What happened to your face?"

"I offended my acupuncturist," said Valentine.

Boots wore her black leather outfit. Clarisse had changed into new denim jeans and a western shirt with a flowered yoke.

"Have a seat, Boots," said Clarisse and waved her casually to the sofa. Boots crossed and sat in the middle. She removed her cap and placed it on the coffee table. Leaning forward she noticed Veronica Lake, who lay on the floor at the other end of the couch.

"Ohhh," smiled Boots, "a Dalmatian!"

"She's an afghan," said Valentine without looking around.

"Hi, doggie." Boots thrust her arm out and wiggled her fingers, but Veronica Lake only sighed heavily and closed her eyes. Boots leaned back and looked about the room. "Nice," she said, "no beams though. You got beams in the bedroom?"

"No," said Valentine, and lowered himself gingerly into a chair beside the fireplace, "but Clarisse has set up a phenomenal system of iron hooks, ropes, and pulleys over the bed. You've never seen anything like it!"

"Oh! Can I see?!" She half rose from the couch, but Clarisse motioned her down again.

"Later Boots," she said, and shot the bolt on the door. "Would you like something to drink?"

"Just water, please."

Clarisse filled a glass in the kitchen, plunked in some ice, and handed it to Boots as she curled on the edge of the sofa. "Well," said Clarisse and stopped.

Boots had unzipped the breast pocket of her jacket, extracted a pill, popped it into her mouth, and washed it down with the entire glass of water. She placed the glass on the end table and stared down at her hands.

"Quaalude?" said Clarisse.

"Just a Valium. Want one?"

Clarisse shook her head.

Valentine was surprised how small the woman was. Her short hair flowed back from her cheeks and softened the sharp lines of her face.

Boots looked up suddenly. "Maybe we ought to get down to business. I shouldn't even have come over—we could have done this all over the phone. I have to get back before Frank comes home. He went to Jamaica Plain to buy some dope—he does that every Saturday—and I've got some errands to do too."

"Has he hit you again?" said Clarisse. She stood on the other side of the fireplace from Valentine.

Boots glanced at Valentine, and then looked away embarrassed. "I don't want to talk about Frank. On the phone you said you and—Valentine—were interested in setting up a meeting with me and Frank. Well, that's fine. Frank's fine when he's working. He wouldn't hit you or anything, so you don't have to worry about that. We respect limits, we always respect limits. You can't make a name in this business if you don't respect limits. So maybe we should set up a date. I brought our calendar along with me." She began to reach into another pocket of her jacket.

"So what kind of limits did Billy Golacinsky have?" asked Valentine. "Pretty wide, if Frank killed him."

Boots looked up slowly, her eyes wide and her brow creased. "Who?"

"That kid who was killed. There was another notice about him in the paper this morning, but all it said was his father had refused to pay burial expenses."

"What are you talking about?"

"Boots," said Valentine, "Frank's been beating you pretty often lately, hasn't he?"

"What do you know about it?"

"You told me," said Clarisse, "that you got that bruise on your arm on Christmas Day. It's not that old, I could tell by the color. You couldn't have gotten it more than a week ago. You were right the first time, you got it on New Year's Day."

Boots said nothing.

Valentine went on: "Somebody we know saw Frank pick up that boy in Park Square the night he was killed, New Year's night. There was a man in the backseat too, and we think it was Searcy. Searcy's been trying to pin this murder on friends of ours, even on me. And Frank's been hitting you to keep you quiet, right?"

Boots stood, but Clarisse went quickly over. With one hand firmly on Boots's arm, she sat and brought Boots down as well.

"I'm getting out of here," said Boots. "You told me you were getting it on with Bill."

Clarisse tightened her grip.

"This is illegal," cried Boots, "this is kidnapping or extortion or something."

"Has Frank been beating you to keep you quiet?" said Clarisse.

"No," said Boots sullenly.

"That's just how he gets his kicks then?" said Valentine.

"No," said Boots, "Frank doesn't hit me."

"You told me..." said Clarisse.

"Bill hits me," said Boots in a low voice.

"Searcy?" cried Valentine. "Searcy hits you?"

"I need another Valium," said Boots. She reached for her pocket but Clarisse stopped her.

"When you've told us everything, then you can have your Valium."

Boots slunk down in the sofa. Clarisse let go her arm and retreated to the fireplace.

"Well," Boots said after a few moments, "I don't know everything."

"Tell us what you do know," said Clarisse.

"Bill came over to the apartment on New Year's night. Bill didn't want to have a session or anything, he just wanted to talk to Frank. But I could tell that he was real mad, so I stayed in the bedroom pretending I was still asleep, even though they were yelling."

"What were they arguing about?" said Valentine.

"Billy Golacinsky."

"Then you did know him," said Clarisse, nodding.

"Yes, but I didn't have anything to do with killing him! Frank did it. Bill told Frank to get Billy out of town. I heard him say that."

"Searcy told Frank to get Billy out of town, and so Frank killed Billy?" said Valentine. "Wasn't that extreme?"

"He said 'get him out of town,' but I think he meant 'kill him.'"

"How did you get mixed up with Billy in the first place?" asked Clarisse.

"Well, one night Frank and I needed a fourth, somebody not to join in but just to take Polaroids for this one client we had who said he wanted a 'pictorial record,' and didn't think he was getting his money's worth unless he had one. So Frank just ran down to the Block and picked up the first kid he saw, and that was Billy."

"When was that?"

"Around Halloween, I guess. Frank gave Billy twenty-five dollars, for an hour's work. Billy really liked it, the money I mean, especially since he didn't even have to have sex for it. Well, that client never came back, but Billy sure did. Like he would stand out on the street and wait till he saw somebody who looked like he was coming up to our place and then he'd show up, like it was coincidence or something. Well, that was all right, sort of, but one night he followed Bill inside. Well, Searcy doesn't like men, but Frank and I were pretty stoned, and then we got Bill stoned, and then Frank made Bill do it with Billy— why does everybody have to be called Bill? Valentine's a nice name, why aren't there more people called Valentine?—and then Billy took some pictures of the three of us. That night we really got into it, hanging from the rafters and all that, and the flash kept going off, and so did we, and then it wasn't going off anymore, and Billy was gone."

"Taking the pictures with him," said Valentine.

"How'd you know?"

"Jeane Dixon predicted it in the *Enquirer*. Then what happened?"

"Well, then Billy came back the next week and said that he didn't take any pictures at all because there wasn't any film and he was just setting the flash off, but we didn't really believe that. Then about a month ago, Billy got busted on the Block. Bill ran into him at the station when he was getting booked and Bill got scared that he'd say something, and so he got the charges dropped. So what does the kid do, instead of going up and thanking Bill?"

"Blackmail," said Clarisse.

Boots nodded. "He came back another time when Bill was there and he said he wanted two hundred dollars—I mean he thought two hundred dollars was a lot of money and he'd be set up for life or something—and Frank went right through the wall, because this kind of thing isn't good for our reputations, you know? So he was screaming at Billy and then Bill hit Billy real hard across the face, he slapped him around. I didn't like that. I'm not into pain, you know what I mean, unless somebody's paying for it. But Billy said he had the pictures and they were in a safe place and he wanted two hundred dollars or he'd take 'em to the police and turn us all in."

"What would he have gained?" said Valentine.

Boots shrugged. "That kid was a real mean zero. It would have made him feel important. So Frank said he could have the money in a week, and Billy said OK."

"When did this happen?" said Valentine.

"Around Christmas."

"And then Searcy told Frank to 'get Billy out of town'?"

Boots nodded. "But he meant for Frank to kill Billy. Because on New Year's Eve, Bill—the cop Bill, I mean—went over to Billy's place on Joy Street and was going to break in or something—because he figured that Billy would be out having a good time on New Year's Eve—but he was too late, because Billy got thrown out that afternoon. So then the next day he tried to find Billy and couldn't and then he came over to our place, real mad and all, and Bill said that they'd ride around the Block and the bus station and find Billy and then they'd get him out of town. So then they left the apartment."

"Was this late?"

"About one o'clock, two o'clock—no wait, it was probably later, because Bill had a bottle with him because he said the bars were closed, so that must have been after two."

"So," said Valentine, "Searcy was the man in the backseat. Figures."

"So anyway," said Boots, having warmed to the story, "Frank came back all by himself all nervous and mad and everything, yelling about Bill, saying that they got that kid out of town all right, but that now he didn't trust Bill, because Bill was a cop, and he told me that if anything happened to him, he'd make sure it happened to me too."

"Accessory after the fact," said Valentine.

Boots nodded. "They hit him in the head with Frank's steering wheel lock, you know, that thing you put on the steering wheel and brake to keep the car from being stolen, it's long and heavy and made of steel or something."

"Which one of them actually killed him?" said Valentine.

"I don't know," said Boots. "Frank said Bill did it, but that's what Frank would say no matter what."

"Why did they dump the body on Scarpetti's lawn?" asked Clarisse.

"Who? I don't know," she shrugged. "Frank just said they were driving around the suburbs where it's dark and quiet, and then they went up the darkest street they could find, and threw the body out the door. Can I have that other Valium now?"

Clarisse nodded, rose, and brought her another glass of water.

Valentine touched the scars on his face lightly. "Boots," he said, "you know that you're going to have to go to the police, don't you?"

"They'll say I did it!"

"No, they won't," said Clarisse, "you'll just turn state's evidence and tell them what you told us, and Frank will confess and Searcy will get his too. You'll probably be in the clear—not completely maybe, but whatever happens you'll be better off than staying with Frank. You know too, don't you, that there's no way that you ought to trust Searcy?"

She nodded reluctantly. "I'm scared," she said simply.

"They could decide—either one of them—that they can't trust you. Does Searcy know that you know about all of this?"

She nodded. "I guess so. I think so."

"Then you're not safe," said Valentine, "see what he did to me last night?"

"I thought you said—" began Boots.

"It was Searcy."

Boots lowered her eyes.

"Well then," said Clarisse brightly, "it's off to District One."

"I have to change clothes first," said Boots.

"What?" Valentine and Clarisse both exclaimed.

Boots fingered the edge of her jacket. "There'll be photographers and if I'm going to be on the front page and on television, then I don't want to be dressed like this. What if Mom sees the picture?"

"There won't be any photographers today," said Valentine. "No television cameras yet. We'll just walk over there. Nobody's expecting us."

"No. I want to put a dress on."

"You think you ought to go back to the apartment?" asked Clarisse. "What if Frank shows up?"

"He won't. He was just about to take off when I left. He always spends the day in Jamaica Plain. He won't be back till dark. He never is."

"OK," said Clarisse, "but Val and I are going with you, and wait with you while you change."

"You don't trust me?"

"Of course we do, going to the police is in your best interests," said Clarisse with a smile, "we just want to make sure that you're all right."

Boots smiled weakly and rose, jamming her hands into the pockets of her jacket. "Will your friend back me up?"

"Who?" said Valentine.

"Your friend who saw Billy get in the car with Frank and Bill. Will he back me up?"

"Yes, of course," said Valentine.

Chapter Twenty-three

VALENTINE AND CLARISSE stood silently while Boots searched her pockets for the keys to the main entrance of the building on Commonwealth. When the woman began checking each pocket a second time, Clarisse rummaged in her leather envelope and brought out the office keys. Just at that moment, Boots Slater found her own in her back pocket, and she held them up smiling.

Valentine and Clarisse followed her closely up to the third floor. As Boots turned her own key in the door, she said, "Come on in and wait, I won't be more than half a second." Valentine nodded and went in right behind her. Clarisse followed and pushed the door closed.

The living room was large but sparsely furnished. A soiled hemp rug covered the floor, and on this were a lumpy sofa with dingy cream-colored upholstery, and two matching armchairs. Several movie magazines and recent copies of *Popular Mechanics* were strewn across a wooden coffee table. Some marijuana was scattered over the open pages of one of the magazines, and a crumpled plastic bag lay to the side.

Clarisse glanced up at the ceiling. "You didn't soundproof this room."

Boots tossed her hat onto a library table that was pushed up between the two windows overlooking Commonwealth Avenue. "Just the workroom," she said. She waved toward the closed door in the back wall.

She stepped toward the bedroom, but stopped when the door to the workroom suddenly shuddered as a large weight was thrown against it. Boots glanced at Valentine and Clarisse with wide frightened eyes. She bolted for the door into the hallway, but Valentine caught her arm. He pushed her toward Clarisse and pointed at the wall.

The doorknob of the closed door rattled as it was turned.

Clarisse grabbed Boots and pulled her to the wall on one side of the door. Valentine pressed against the wall on the other side.

The door flew open and Frank Hougan ran into the room, his chin bloody from a gash in his lower lip. He headed straight for the door to the hallway.

Lieutenant William Searcy stumbled into the room after him, only a couple of feet beyond Clarisse. His revolver was raised and he aimed at Frank with an unsteady and white-bandaged hand. He pulled the trigger, and the explosion was horrifyingly loud. Jerking backward and buckling at the knees, Frank smashed against a chair. He fell to the floor, and blood from his wounded thigh poured out over the hemp rug.

Searcy aimed the gun again.

Boots screamed and pressed her face against the wall.

Searcy snapped his head around; his eyes were blood-shot, his hair rumpled and damp, and a heavy shadow of beard streaked his face. In one swift motion Clarisse swung her envelope up, hitting Searcy's hand with such force that the gun whirled into the air, clunking to the floor behind him. The latch of the envelope broke and papers flew up around his face.

Valentine dove at Searcy, driving his shoulder hard into the policeman's back. Searcy fell forward, stiff-legged, his chest and face slamming into the hemp rug. Clarisse jumped out of the way, bruising her shin badly on the corner of the coffee table.

Valentine jumped on the policeman's back, driving his knees into Searcy's sides. He grabbed the man's wrists and twisted his arms back and up, grinding them between his shoulder blades. When Searcy tried to push up, Valentine yanked his wrists violently. The man cried out in pain, and collapsed.

Clarisse limped over to the revolver and picked it up. She held it before her with both hands, aiming at Searcy's head. Valentine looked up.

"Don't point that thing at me!" cried Valentine, staring into the barrel of the gun.

Frank jerked convulsively and Clarisse fanned the gun toward him. Grabbing the arm of the chair he struggled to pull himself up. Blood poured out of the wound high up on his right thigh. The pain was too great and he let go, falling back onto the floor and groaning.

There were loud footsteps in the hallway, and a female voice called out, "Marjorie, call the police! My phone's out!"

Boots twisted against the wall. She drew her trembling hands down slowly from her face. "They have a witness," she gasped, "they have a witness and they saw you pick up Billy!"

Frank raised his head from the floor. He tried to shout something, but the effort was too great and he fell to bleating again.

"They can prove you did it!" Boots cried. She pushed away from the wall and darted toward the bedroom.

"Where are you going?" shouted Valentine, and pulled at Searcy's arms, so that he cried out again.

"The cops are coming!" Boots yelled. "I got to change clothes."

"No!" Clarisse shrieked. "You don't have to change now!"

"I'll be right back!" She ran into the bedroom. Valentine sighed and tried to make himself comfortable on the small of Searcy's back. "She's stoned out of her mind," said Valentine softly.

"I didn't kill anybody!" Searcy gasped, and tried to raise himself.

Valentine leaned close to his face. "It hasn't been for want of trying," he said. "You just put a bullet in Hougan's leg, and you gave me a taste of your technique last night, but it looks like your only success was a nineteen-year-old kid—"

"I didn't touch that kid!"

"Don't try to convince me—" said Valentine. He broke off, and turned to Clarisse. "I've got him, Hougan can't do anything, call the police, but don't put the gun down."

Clarisse nodded, and edged toward the phone, which was on a small stand beside the door into the bedroom. She punched "911" and stuck the receiver between her shoulder and her ear.

Hougan was arched over the arm of the sofa, gnashing his teeth in pain.

"You may not have killed Billy Golacinsky," said Valentine to Searcy, "but you sure as hell knew what really happened to him. *That's* why your investigation was so rotten. You weren't trying to find out who did it—you were just making sure that no one knew that *you* had any connection with it. That's what Professor Lawrence—"

"How'd—" began Searcy, but when Clarisse began to talk on the phone, Valentine jerked the policeman's arms, so that he broke off in pain.

"My name is Lovelace," said Clarisse loudly, "there's been a shooting. One man is injured, and the other is being held down. We need police and an ambulance as soon as you can get them here." She gave the address and the apartment number. She hung up after a moment and said. "They're on their way. Good old Marjorie upstairs must have already called in."

"You fags—!" breathed Searcy.

"Anyway," Valentine went on lightly, "Professor Lawrence said that you seemed more interested in finding out that he didn't see anything New Year's night, than in hearing what he *did* see. And it's also why most of your investigation has been done when you were off duty, and alone. We assumed that it was just Scarpetti, down on your back, but you were out to protect yourself. Were you even on this investigation at all?"

"Yes—"

Valentine twisted his arm again, and went on. "But then you started looking around to see who you could pin this on easiest, trying to find some squishy faggot who knew Billy, but it turned out there weren't any more squishy faggots in Boston. You—"

Boots appeared in the doorway. She'd removed her leather jacket. Her arms were raised as she pulled a brown woolen dress over her head. She had not taken off either her leather pants or boots. She stared at Frank as she feverishly worked with the button at the back of the collar. "I'm going to turn state's evidence! Just like Linda Kasabian! I'm going to—"

Frank yelled inarticulately.

Sirens wailed outside on Commonwealth.

"Here come the cops!" cried Boots. "I'll be ready as soon as I get on my makeup!"

"Boots, for Christ's sake..." Clarisse sighed.

Without bothering to hook up the zipper, Boots retreated to the bedroom. "I won't need a lawyer or anything!" she called out.

"Get out here!" demanded Valentine.

"Just a minute!" she cried.

Boots appeared again in the doorway. She held a comb in one hand and a tube of lipstick in the other.

Clarisse glanced at Boots for a second, and then swung the gun about and aimed directly at her. "Get over by Frank," she said.

"What...?" Boots stammered.

Clarisse pulled back the hammer. "Do it," she said coldly. She held the gun steady as she tracked Boots with it. The woman stepped carefully around Searcy to stand beside Frank.

"You said I could be state's evidence!" she cried. "I—"

"Clarisse..." Valentine asked, confused.

"It was you in the backseat New Year's night," said Clarisse.

"No! It was Frank and Bill. I was—"

"No!" cried Searcy. "I wasn't there!"

"You killed Billy," said Clarisse, staring at Boots.

The comb dropped out of her hand. Frank swatted at her legs maliciously and then doubled up in pain. Boots stepped wildly back, and fell onto the couch.

"It was you who killed Billy," said Clarisse again.

"It was an accident! Billy was yelling and hitting Frank and screaming about wanting money and those Polaroids and..." She gulped air. She stared down at Frank's wounded leg and seemed for a few moments to forget herself. She picked up more calmly then. "...and I was speeding my brains out, and Billy was hitting Frank, and we nearly ran off the road, and Frank grabbed Billy and shoved him back over the seat, and then Billy started screaming at me, telling me to give him money, and he reached out and grabbed me, he grabbed my shoulders, and he started shaking me, and..." Boots seemed to lose herself again.

"And *what?*" demanded Valentine.

Frank continued to groan loudly.

"...he grabbed me and he was hurting me, and the crook-lock was on the backseat, so I picked it up and swung it at his face to make him let go of me, and then there was all this blood, so I threw the crook-lock out the window and then we had to go back and pick it up because Frank said he wasn't going to buy another one and—"

Searcy abruptly jerked his legs up. Valentine lost his balance and fell sideways. Searcy's wrists slipped from his grip as he tumbled backward.

Confused shouts filled the hallway outside and a high-pitched voice yelled "Police!"

As Valentine came to his feet, Searcy pushed him hard against Clarisse. The gun fired toward the ceiling as she fell back against the door, Valentine tripping over her feet. Searcy grabbed the gun and stepped back, pointing the barrel point-blank at them. Both jumped aside in opposite directions. He fired and the door splintered just above Clarisse's shoulder.

Boots screamed again. Searcy turned toward her, the gun still raised. Valentine threw the hallway door open wide.

Chapter Twenty-four

VALENTINE STOOD on the landing with his back to the open apartment door. Clarisse sat sideways on the stairs leading to the top floor. She leaned her head against the wall and smoked, a little nervously. The runner beneath their feet was littered with splinters of wood. Another door on the hallway was open a crack and two young women peered out, neither saying anything. Two policemen had just disappeared around the stairs that led down, with handcuffed Searcy between them.

A woman with long blond hair leaned far over the railing above. "Clarisse!" she hissed, "what the hell happened down there?"

Clarisse looked up. "Domestic quarrel," she answered shortly. The woman whistled and disappeared from the stairs.

Clarisse nodded in the direction of the door behind Valentine, and he turned around. Two paramedics angled a stretcher into the hallway. Frank Hougan's leg had been hastily bandaged and he lay with one arm flung across his eyes; it was apparent he had been given some kind of painkiller.

"How'd you know it was Boots who killed Billy?" demanded Valentine.

"I didn't," said Clarisse, "I only knew it wasn't Frank."

"What do you mean?"

"It was the right side of Billy's head that was caved in. If Frank had hit the boy while he was driving, he would have hit him on the left side."

"But if the kid had been turned around screaming at Boots in the backseat then his right side would have been toward Frank."

"But Frank couldn't hit anybody hard enough to kill him at the same time he was driving, so it had to be whoever was in the backseat."

"Yes," said Valentine, "but what if they had stopped the car, and gotten out, and that's where Frank hit him over the head and killed him?"

Clarisse paused. "I didn't think of that." She brightened. "But I was right, so it doesn't matter really, does it?"

"But the question is, how did you know it was Boots in the backseat and not Searcy?" argued Valentine. "Trudy said she saw two *men* in the car."

Clarisse laughed. "Val, even *you* mistook Boots for a man, and that was at pretty short range. Besides, it didn't make sense for Searcy to be in that car."

"Why not?"

"Searcy's a cop. You don't think he'd be stupid enough to be in a car that was circling the Block and the bus station at three in the morning, with police headquarters a block away, and squad cars going through there all the time?"

"I guess not," admitted Valentine. "But maybe if he had wanted to get rid of the kid bad enough, if he thought his whole career depended on having the kid out of the way..."

Clarisse nodded. "I wasn't sure till she came out of the bedroom the second time, putting on her makeup."

"What? She didn't say a word then—she just said she wasn't going to need a lawyer."

Clarisse pointed over Valentine's shoulder.

A policeman was leading Boots out the door, and Valentine regarded her closely. Her hair fell across her forehead, and the light eye shadow she'd applied was already streaked. She stared at them with vague unemotional eyes, and took a short noisy breath. Her lips were bright with vermilion lipstick.

"She must have got the lipstick on him sometime that night, either playing around with him or by accident, and then he wiped it off on his handkerchief, or maybe she just borrowed it when she was putting it on," said Valentine.

"Who knows?" shrugged Clarisse. "But when I saw that, I realized that she had been with Billy that night and that she had lied to us. And if it had been Hougan who killed the boy, then Boots wouldn't have lied to us about being in the car. She must have thought she was going to get away with it."

"Well," said Valentine, "I guess we have to go down to District One, and clear all this up. I'd love to be the one to break the news to Scarpetti that the 'homosexual conspirators' in this case were a straight couple and a Boston cop."

"That's some comfort," said Clarisse, standing. She put an arm around Valentine's shoulder. "Let's do something."

"What?"

"After we finish things off at the police station, let's go have a few stiff drinks, cry over our plight, and then call TWA and book ourselves on the first flight to Key West."

"I am not about to put this bruised and broken body out on the beach for all those tanned good-looking *uninjured* men to laugh at."

Clarisse sighed and pulled her coat up. A policeman waited to escort them down.

"You still want the drinks though?" Valentine said.

"Honey, I just got a pistol fired at my face!" She shoved the leather envelope under her arm. "In the immortal words of Mildred Pierce, 'Let's get stinko!'"